DOPE BOY

ATL

Introduction

R eal talk Shawty, I can't stand these fake ass rappers! nigga's talking 'bout bussing they gun and marking niggas.

Lying ass niggas up in the studio safe and sound while a nigga like me out in them streets for real!

Got G.B.I., F.B.I., D.E.A. breathing down a nigga's neck. Fuckin' Mexicans that will kill ya whole family 'bout they bread. Got beef with niggas cross town. At war with them New York niggas.

Y'all don't see me up in no studio tryna rap. So why them fuck niggas all up in they video flexing like they moving keys.

Stay up in the studio where it's safe. Trust me, it's real in the field! Dope Boy for real!

Table of Contents

CHAPTER

1

TRAP STAR Cameron Forrest was born and raised in Decatur, Georgia, a sprawling suburb just east of Atlanta. Don't let the word suburb fool you because 'The Dec' is as hood as it gets.

Its main thoroughfares Glenwood and Candler roads were just as notorious as Flatbush or Long Beach Blvd. in Brooklyn and Compton.

There were so many murders that they don't even make the news anymore, except for when the sheriff killed his successor for winning the election. That's Hood!

Cam was born to a fast ass fourteen year old named Tywanna. They lived with her mother Linda and sister Satira in the Eastwyck Townhomes on Candler Rd.

Eastwyck was a sprawling development containing over 400 units spread across its 200 acres. Their apartment was a small but immaculate three bedroom unit in the back of the complex.

It consisted of a living room, kitchen and bathroom on the first floor, with three small bedrooms on the top floor. The coolest part was the basement that doubled as a laundry room and play room.

Despite the fact that Cam's grandmother Linda was an upright church lady, her daughters were lost to the streets. Ebony, at 16, had a 35 year old boyfriend, and 14 year old Tywanna had a baby.

By the time Ebony was 18 she too had a son to add to the chaos of the house. Linda was always fussing at her wayward daughters in hopes of straightening them out.

Young Tywanna stayed in the streets so much Cameron's first words were 'Momma will be back'. He hated to see his mother leave but knew there was no yelling when she was gone.

She spent so much time in the streets until she finally just stopped coming home. Ebony's son Fernando moved in the room and the boys were inseparable.

Some two years later Tywanna came to claim her child, and fireworks flew.

"Girl what you mean you here to get your son?" Linda asked.

"That's what I said," Tywanna shot back, "I got me an apartment, and got me a check but Cam gotta live there so I don't get cut off!"

"You ain't even seen him in two years! He don't even know you," Linda pleaded.

"Well that's my son, and I'm getting food stamps for him so…" she said smartly.

In the end, Cam's grandmother had no legal standing and he went with his mother. The apartment was located in a rundown complex on Glenwood Rd.

It had two bedrooms which gave Cam his own room for the first time in his short live. Tywanna made an effort to take care of her child and fixed his room up nicely.

He had a race car bed with sheet sets that matched the curtains. A small TV and video game system provided the entertainment.

Since it was the last summer before his first day of school his closet was full of nice new clothes that he couldn't wear no matter how much he begged. Life was good, for a time.

Tywanna did well not to hang out in the streets but soon the streets began to hang out at her apartment. At first just and her girlfriends smoking and listening to music.

Depending on the time of day, Cam either got sent outside to play or to his room. If he got bored he would sneak out and spy on his mother and friends from the hallway. He liked hearing their banter and watching them sing and dance along with the latest songs.

Cam got more than he bargained for one night. Tywanna and one of her boyfriends were going at it pretty hot and heavy on the sofa. He stifled a giggle when they both stripped and fucked in front of him.

The sex act fascinated young Cameron and imbedded in his psyche. The shit looked fun and he couldn't wait to try it. Since Tywanna had a couple suitors, Cam saw various sex acts on a regular.

CHAPTER

2

T ywanna limited her drug use to weed, beer and the occasional x-pill. From his stealthy position, young Cam pretended to smoke and drink along with the company. One night he was present while his mother and friend Tina tried cocaine for the first time.

They took turns snorting lines off the glass coffee table.

"Gurl! This shit fire!" Tywanna exclaimed as she straightened up from the table.

"Mmm hmm, that nigga Tye hooked me up!" Tina sang before bending over to inhale two lines of her own.

They continued snorting until the small pile was gone. Of course the inevitable question was as by Tywanna. "You ain't got no more?" She inquired eagerly.

"Gurl no!" Tina said sounding wounded. "I ain't got no money left either."

"Man I got fifty dollars, but that's for Cam's game. His birthday tomorrow," Tywanna said desperately.

"Straight then!" Tina announced as if the last of her winning lottery numbers was called.

"Tye got some fat ass twentys! You still gone have thirty dollars!"

Tywanna went for it and spent twenty of her last fifty on blow. A few hours later she spent twenty of her last thirty on blow again.

The next day instead of heading over to South DeKalb Mall for games. Tywanna pulled her angry son off the bus at the top of Eastwyck. Cameron was hot about not getting his video games but eager to see his grandmother and little cousin.

"Hey girl," a group of girls called to Tywanna as they descended the first hill of the complex.

"What's up gurl!" Tywanna sang. "I'm finna drop Cam off and come back."

Grandma Linda and her daughter argued about where the fifty she gave her for Cam's birthday went. Tywanna left in a huff which is what she wanted to do anyway.

"Come on boy," Linda ordered and piled her grandsons into the car. A short time later they were entering Walmart where Cam picked out his first bike.

Back at home she fixed a huge meal complete with a cake. Tywanna was a no show for two days.

Not sure if her daughter cooked, Linda grabbed a kid's meal from the hamburger joint across from the apartments when she dropped Cam off at home. She was still salty about the stunt Tywanna pulled so she simply honked the horn when she pulled up to the front door.

Cam's mother opened the door and waved him in, not wanting to tangle either.

"Hey Lil Man," she sang, giving him a kiss on his mouth.

"This my friend Tye, go to your room," Tywanna said as he entered.

Cam looked at the well dressed man and then to the pile of coke on the table. He followed orders and went to his room to eat.

When boredom set in Cam set out to spy on his mother and friend. He was astounded to see his mother giving the man head.

"Suck that dick Shawty," Tye ordered standing over Tywanna.

When Tye climaxed he held Tywanna's head and forced her to take every drop. As soon as he released his grip she took off to the bathroom.

Cam snuck back to bed passing his gagging, spitting mother kneeled at the toilet. He climbed back into his car and went to sleep.

"Mama!" Cam said nudging his sleeping mother. "Mama I'm hungry."

"Boy eat that cereal," she said rolling back over to resume her much needed sleep.

"Ain't no milk," Cam protested.

"You better put some water in and leave me alone!" she demanded.

Tywanna slept the day away while Cam took his new bike out for a spin. Cam shared his ride with his closest friend Bobby even though he was warned not to.

Bobby befriended Cam from day one in the complex. He spent the whole day with them even eating dinner since Tywanna stayed sleep the whole day.

It was dark when Cameron got home so Bobby's dad walked him and helped him bring his bike in.

He woke his mom up let her know he was home, expecting to be in trouble. Luckily Tywanna felt guilty at neglecting her child all day.

She and Bobby's dad flirted when they met as Cam looked on.

"Come here little man," Tywanna sang spreading her arms.

Cam took her up on the affection and rushed into her arms. It was a touching mother son moment until Tywanna kissed him and he recalled Tye's dick in her mouth. He frowned up and tried to pull away from the kisses.

"Oh you too big to kiss your mama," she teased planting wet kisses all over his face.

CHAPTER

3

Tywanna's drug use slowly increased until she was getting high in one way or another all day everyday. Her guy friends might come smoke weed hoping to hit or girlfriends to share their drugs.

Still she managed to hold onto some semblance of being a good mom. Ultimately the lure of the streets won out.

"Girl let's hit da club," Sherry sang winding her hips to the jam on the radio.

"Mmm hmm, girl that sexy ass D-lite 'posed to perform and you know he gone put on!" Tina co-signed.

Y'all know I caint go nowhere," Tywanna whined. "Cam in the sleep."

"Shit, if he sleep he ain't gone even know we gone," Tina reasoned.

"For real though!" Sherry cheered, "Ain't like that lil nigga need a bottle."

"Y'all think he gonna be ok?" Tywanna asked seeking a little more approval.

"Girl yes!" Sherry laughed before bending to snort the last of the cocaine off the table.

Realizing that that was the last of the dope, and that she would be stuck home alone Tywanna gave in.

"OK, gimmee a second. Let me change!" she said taking off towards the back. She returned two minutes later in a short skirt and cheap sandals.

"Girl you look good!" Tina said reaching for her cheap shoes as well.

"Let me check on my baby," Tywanna said before slipping into her son's room.

"Mama be back," she said quietly before kissing his forehead.

The familiar phrase stirred Cam but by the time he awoke fully, the apartment was empty. With nothing better to do he went to investigate. He sipped a warm can of beer and pretended he was smoking the butts in the ashtray.

He didn't he had fell asleep until he heard his mother and company at the door. Since he didn't have enough time to make it to his room he ducked behind the sofa.

Cam was stuck as his mother, Tina and two guys they met in the club stumbled in. He remained motionless as they drank and smoked. Finally one of the men went with Tywanna to her room. As soon as they cleared the room the remaining couple stripped.

Cameron amused himself watching the man fuck Tina in several positions. His mind shot to Trish, Bobby's sister. She was a year older than him and Bobby but he swore then he would marry her one day. If not, at least hit her from the back like dude had Tina.

Growing bored and tired he slipped into his room and back in bed. It was no surprise that Tywanna was still sleep in the morning when her son got up. At five he was already more mature than kids twice his age. His mother too.

He poured the right amount of water on his cereal and ate breakfast. He drug his bike out and began his day.

Over the next few weeks Tywanna was turning small scale tricks for her new drug of choice, crack. Dealers would come through and drop off a few sacks in exchange for some head or tail.

Since motherhood took a backseat to getting high, young Cameron was often hungry. Sometimes one of the men who visited his mother threw him a few bucks. Cam, wise beyond his years began to stash some for hard times.

For food he generally cut through the path between the complex and came out at Mr. Wright's store. Mr. Wright was an old man who looked angry all the time, but had a heart of gold. His gruff demeanor betrayed his true character.

Cam made sure to share with Bobby and Trish whenever he could. He spent more and more time with them and less at home.

When summer came to a close, Grandma Linda scooped Cam up to spend a weekend. She noticed the boy had lost weight and seemed hardened. She pried and pried but Cam's loyalty to his mother kept him silent.

Again, not wanting to enter her daughter's home Linda honked her horn to announce her presence.

A disheveled Tywanna came to the door squinting as if allergic to sunlight. The first thing Cam noticed was the familiar sweet sickly smell of crack. The next thing he noticed was nothing. There was nothing left in the apartment.

Gone was the T.V. and small stereo. Even the cheap living room set was gone.

"Where's out stuff Mama?" Cam pleaded desperately.

"Someone took our stuff," Tywanna replied meekly unable to look at him as she spoke.

Cam's mind raced to his room and he followed it into his now empty space. His T.V. and video game was gone! So was his race car bed. Even the new clothes were 'stolen'.

He sank to the floor and sulked. He didn't cry like the average five year old would. His heart was now too hard for crying.

"Don't worry, mama gone get you all new stuff when my check come," Tywanna said sweetly.

She knew she wouldn't and so did he. If and when a check came it too would be smoked and they both knew it.

CHAPTER

4

School was hell for young Cam without new clothes. Even in the most impoverished ghettos in America kids wore new clothes for the first day of school.

The two bright sides of it were the breakfast and lunch programs and math. Cam loved both. His teachers noticed he had the mind of a budding mathematician.

He also secretly wished school lasted until dinner so he could eat that as well. Quite a few times he had to settle for whatever scraps Tywanna could throw together.

Once he cried so much from the hunger his mother was forced to react.

"Come on, Damn!" she said as if his hunger was an inconvenience.

He followed her through to the path and came out at Mr. Wright's store. Cam watch with curiosity as his mother put food items in her clothes. He alternated between looking at her and looking at Mr. Wright.

Instead of stopping at the counter Tywanna led her son out the door past a grim faced Mr. Wright. Cam knew his mother was stealing and he knew the owner saw her and if confused him.

Tywanna couldn't resist trying her luck with one of the young dealers peddling their wares outside.

"You straight," she asked one who had frequented rented space in her body for dope.

"I'm cool," he frowned turning up his nose.

Tywanna turned away dejected until two of the other dealers approached.

"Say Shawty what you tryna do?" one asked knowingly.

"I'ma take care of you if you break me off," she said seductively as if her five year old wasn't standing there. As if he five year old son didn't understand that his mother intended to let the man have his way with her in exchange for a few of the rocks she seemed to love so much.

"That's what's up, my boy too?" the dealer asked pointing to his friend.

Tywanna hesitated for a second at the notion of her first train. Only for a second before leading the men to her apartment.

Once at home Tywanna opened the cans of pasta and green beans. Since the gas had been turned off she dumped it into a bowl and sent her son to his room to eat.

Cam scarfed the food down until the sounds of laughter wafted to his ears. Curiosity again led him to see yet another sex act.

The two men had his mother naked on the floor each inside of her. They giggled hysterically as they slammed into her from her front and back. If Tywanna wasn't affected by the act her son sure was.

The act was so aggressive Cam wanted to pull them off her. Pull them out of her. Luckily for all, the men finished at the same time, both pulling out and ejaculating on her.

They grinned wildly as they sprayed her face and hair with semen. Each tossed a couple of small blue baggies on the floor and left.

Without even cleaning herself off Tywanna tore into a baggie and smoked the contents. Cam went back to his room to finish his cold food. Cold food went well with his now cold heart.

The scene repeated itself night after night. She stole food to feed he child and sold herself to feed her addiction.

Men of all sorts came day and night. All kinds of men – old, young, white, black. Even Bobby's dad occasionally came by for sex.

Cam decided to add to the haul on the next trip to Mr. Wright's store. As his mother concealed pasta, and vegetables, he went after candy and cakes.

The two of them were loaded down as they walked past a stone faced Mr. Wright. Again, he saw them steal, but again said nothing.

Cam had more candy than he could eat and formulated a plan. He saw what kind of business the local candy lady did and decided he'd do the same.

The next day he sold his cakes and candy and came home with four dollars. His plan was to save it for rainy day but when his mother hadn't come home hunger pains force him outside.

It has been so long since he ate at the McDonald's across the street, the golden arches seemed to be calling his name.

After looking left, right, then left again he ventured out to cross Glenwood Road.

"Get ya lil ass out the street," a lady screamed as she swerved to avoid him.

His heart was pounding with fear as he reached the counter. He paid for his own meal and sat by a window to enjoy the view as he ate. Cam took a bite of his burger and almost choked on it as Tywanna stopped right in front of the large window.

She had her back to him as she waved at the passing cars. When one stopped she darted out in traffic almost as recklessly as her son did minutes earlier and got in with the stranger.

Cam wolfed down the rest of his happy meal and headed home. His mother hadn't returned by morning. Fortunately, he had long been getting himself ready for school.

CHAPTER

5

"Say Shawty, let me get some of dat candy," Octavius, the school yard bully balked at Cam.

"Nothing left," Cam replied having just sold his last.

"So let me get some of that money then," Octavius demanded closing the distance between them.

Cam knew Octavius bullied half the school and refused to go out without a fight. As soon as the larger kid got close enough Cameron fired off.

He took a beating that day. And the next, and the one after that. Cam fought him everyday and never won. He also never gave up. Never lost his dinner money, candy, or heart.

Tywanna was scarcely seen so Cam had to fend for himself. He trekked through the path to Mr. Wright's store to steak food for dinner and inventory for school.

As usual Mr. Wright mean mugged him as he loaded up. He was so busy stuffing his clothes and pockets he hadn't noticed Mr. Wright's approach.

"Boy why you keep stealing from me!" Mr. Wright demanded, snatching him by the arm. "Can't tell your mama, shit she steal more than you."

When Cam couldn't pull away from the man's grip he broke down crying.

"Aight, aight, stop yo crying boy," Mr. Wright said somewhat softly. "I know you can't be eating all that candy you be taking. What you do give it away?" Trick with the lil girls. Let me find out you a trick."

"No sir, I ain't no trick," Cam said defiantly even though he had no idea what he meant. "I sell it at school."

"So where yo money at?" Mr. Wright asked now curious.

"I hid it so my mama can't find it," he said.

"Well you can't be stealing so come on," the old man said. He led him in the back and handed him a broom.

"Go out there and sweep the lot, you gotta earn ya keep," he said.

As Cameron swept he saw his mother hop out of one car and into another before both feet hit the ground solid. That would be the last time he saw her that week.

"Hey! there's my lil man," Tywanna sang cheerfully as Cam came in from playing. "Give mama a kiss."

Cam went over and gave his mother his cheek to kiss.

"I'm sorry baby, mama missed you," she said planting kisses on him.

Cam showed no emotion and didn't return the display of affection. He just prayed she didn't take his food or money.

Later that night Cam listened in as Tywanna filled her friend Sherry in on her whereabouts.

"Girl, I done messed around and got locked up!" she said cheerfully.

"Un uh! For what?" Sherry asked while preparing to load her shooter.

"Trying to catch me a trick! Turned out to be damn police," she explained.

"You shoulda just sucked his dick!" Sherry said as if that was the answer to every problem.

"Girl I tried. Nigga talking he married and shit! I'm like so! Half dem niggas out there married! A nigga still wanna get his dick sucked!" Tywanna exclaimed.

"I know that's right," Sherry cosigned as she exhaled her hit. "Guess bitches stop sucking dick once they get married."

"Shit I was in there three days, without a blast. I went over to see Tye and took his whole bomb!" Tywanna bragged, producing a large bag filled with individual blue bags.

"Girl! He gone kill you!" Sherry exclaimed.

"Uh uh, girl he a trick too," Tywanna laughed. "Suck him off and we straight."

Cam came home the next day to find his mother secluded in her room. She barked instruction to go get food from Mr. Wright when he asked for dinner.

As he prepared to leave he saw Tye pull up out front. Delighted to see him, hoping for the dollar or two Tye always threw him Cam raced to tell his mother.

"Mama! Mama Tye out front! he said knocking on the door.

Tywanna snatched the door open butt naked with a look of sheer horror pasted on her face.

"Don't open the door!" she yelled in a whisper.

Cam looked past her to the naked man on the bed. The man lifted the pipe to his mouth and took a sizzling hit.

"You hear me boy! Don't open that door!" she stressed again shaking him by his shoulders.

Tye yelled and banged on the door for several minutes before getting back in his car. He pulled off only to return a few minutes later to try again.

It was over an hour later when the coast was clear enough to go out. Most five year old would have been too scared to walk through the path after dusk but not Cameron. Nothing scared him.

"Boy what you doing out this late?" Mr. Wright asked when the child walked in. "Where your mama?"

Home, she sent me to get something to ear," Cam said.

"Turk hold it down. I'll be back," Mr. Wright said to the clerk. He took his young friend to McDonalds and then home.

Mr. Wright had grown attached to the young boy. He schooled him on the art of hustling. Mr. Wright showed him how and when to order and what. Showed him how to save some money and invest some.

As a result, Cam's little candy business was doing quite well. Now instead of stealing he had to re-up like any other retailer would. At five he could explain the difference between wholesale and retail. He know about profit margins, capital and credit. Young Cam was a hustler.

CHAPTER

6

T ywanna had managed to duck Tye for weeks and began to let her guard down. When Sherry came to smoke with her she greedily accepted the offer.

The familiar blue baggies gave her pause but her addiction urged her on. They shared hits over the six pack of cheap beer Sherry supplied. As soon as Tywanna went to use the bathroom her guest discretely unlocked the front door and pulled out her cell phone.

"Come on," she whispered and hung up as her host returned.

Young Cam heard the voices and to go be nosey. Seeing it was only Sherry, he was about to ease away until he saw the front door slowly open.

Tywanna hadn't even noticed it until Tye was crossing the threshold. She violently coughed up the hit she was holding for dear life.

"What's up Shawty?" Tye said with a sinister grin.

"Hey baby! I been looking all over for you," Tywanna said nervously.

Sherry sprang to her feet and grabbed her purse and remaining beer.

"Here Shawty," Tye said handing her a handful of the small blue bags.

Sherry slipped them into her purse and left without a word or backward glance.

"Much as I did for you, you gone steal from me," Tye growled approaching Tywanna.

"Baby I'm sorry!" Tywanna pleaded. "Let me make it up to you. Lemme work it off."

She dropped to the floor and scrambled to get his dick out of his pants and into her mouth. She punctuated the blow by apologizing periodically.

Tye slowly eased his belt from around his waist as she blew him. Cam chuckled inwardly at the thought of his mother getting a whooping.

Tye didn't whoop Tywanna. Instead he slipped the belt around her neck. A sick smile spread across his face as he pulled the noose tight.

Tywanna stopped sucking and reached for the belt. She tried in vain to remove death from her neck.

Cam watched helplessly as his mother was choked to death. He and Tye made eye contact as he released the belt and let his victim fall over. He calmly put the belt back on and walked out.

Not knowing what else to do Cam went back to bed. In the morning he passed his dead mother and went to see Mr.

Wright. He stood in line while Mr. Wright handled his morning rush.

"Boy why you not in school?" Mr. Wright asked between customers.

"My mama dead," he replied plainly.

"What?" Mr. Wright replied unsure if he heard what he heard.

"My mama dead," Cam repeated. "On the floor."

"Turk! Take over!" Mr. Wright demanded rushing from behind the counter. He took Cam by the hand and rushed him into his truck.

"Wait here!" he barked when they reached the apartment. It only took a few seconds for him to confirm that Tywanna was no longer among the living.

He shook his head at the sight of the dead girl. His face was masked with anger as he dialed 911. Moments later the first of many police cars pulled to a stop in front of the apartment.

Cam watched a flurry of activity from the truck until his grandmother pulled up. She went in the apartment and rushed out in tears. She was hysterical until Mr. Wright pointed out her grandson.

"Oh my God baby are you OK?" she asked practically snatching him from the truck. She pulled him close squeezing him tightly. Linda pushed him back enough to inspect him then hugged him again.

His mind was screamin, "Tye killed my mama!!" but he said nothing. No matter how many times was asked he said nothing.

Cam was seated in his grandmother's car while his mother was carried out in a black body bag. Once the crime scene was cleared, Linda went in to see what she could salvage. She came out empty handed.

Cam's grandmother fought not to cry but the sight of the apartment overwhelmed her. She couldn't believe the squalor her daughter and grandson were living in.

She'd seen the crack pipes and drug paraphernalia the police removed. Knew her child had been murdered.

What she didn't know is what ill effects the last few months would have had on her grandson. Didn't know it turned him into a beast.

CHAPTER

7

"**D**umb bitch! Told her ass!" Ebony fumed before bursting into tears. She was in the process of dressing herself and son for her sister's funeral.

She alternated between grief and anger at not being able to save her only sibling. Cam sat on the sofa fully dressed staring off into space.

Every time he closed his eyes he could see Tye choking the life out of his mother. When it was quiet enough he could hear her struggle to stay alive as the noose tightened around her neck.

"Come on girl, we gone be late," Linda said sticking her head into Ebony's room.

"We coming!" Ebony shot back in disgust.

"Chile, I know you upset, but making me jump on you for being disrespectful ain't gone help nothing," Linda replied.

Ebony sucked her teeth and snatched young Fernando off the bed. "Come on!" she demanded pulling him to the stairs.

The grieving family rode up Candler Road in silence. Tywanna's funeral was to be held in the same church she'd been baptized in only a few short years before.

One of the sisters from the church had her funeral there a week earlier and the placed was packed. So the now empty pews rattled Linda. Even young Cam knew there should be more people.

Where were all those men now? The ones who couldn't stay out of Tywanna. The one who sold her dope. Where was Sherry and Tina? Where was Tye.

The preacher preached a beautiful sermon about a girl he didn't know. Linda cried causing her two grandsons to cry. Ebony silently fumed with her lip poked out.

Cam, at five, daydreamed about one day choking Tye and seeing him laying in a box. Watching his family grieve. The thought caused smile to spread across his face.

Finally the family, Mr. Wright and a few of the older church folk who loved a good funeral filed past the casket for one final look. Tywanna looked nothing like the large picture along side the casket. The picture portrayed a lovely young lady; full of life, full of potential, with a bright smile. While inside the box lay a shriveled, ashen, stranger that caused Linda's knees to buckle. Ebony gasped loudly at the sight and finally broke all the way down. Mr. Wright had to help them both maintain their stance.

The small solemn procession proceeded across the street to the nondescript grave site. No one actually heard anything the preacher said. They were all engrossed in their own thoughts.

A final flower was laid on the low budget casket before it was lowered into the ground. No one could bare to watch dirt being tossed on top so they turned away, then walked away leaving Tywanna behind with the dead.

CHAPTER

8

C ameron had only been gone a few months, but returned a different person. The amount of sex and violence he'd witnessed was a lot for his young mind to process.

His grandmother had replaced all his clothes, toys and games, but nothing could repair the damage done inside. Only time would tell how it would alter not just him, but Atlanta as well.

Cam rode the school bus with a bunch of loud rowdy children to his new school. This would be a new experience for him with new friends, new teachers and no Octavius.

Just like before, he set up shop selling candy and came home with a pocket full of money. He wasn't sure what his next move would be since he couldn't replenish his supply.

Mr. Wright had schooled the boy, not just about business but how to hustle. There is a difference. A hustler doesn't need a particular product, the whole world is open.

Mr. Wright was an old vet from Blick City, New Jersey so he recognized young Cam's drive instantly. As any vet will tell you hustling can't be taught. You're either born a hustler or you're not.

As the school bus descended into the apartment complex, Cam saw his Aunt Ebony and cousin Fernando walking to the store. He quickly got off at the first step and caught up to them.

While Ebony selected overpriced goods from the stores aisles Cam went to talk business.

"Excuse sir," he announced as soon as the Arab clerk had a reprieve from the register.

"Yes little fellow," Ali replied both amused and taken aback by the polite manner of the child. Most of the kids ran around like wild banshees waiting for him to blink so they could steal something.

"I need to buy some candy, wholesale," he explained.

"Wholesale?" Ali laughed, then called his brother over. A brief dialog in Arabic caused the other man to laugh as well.

Unfazed, Cam went on to explain his little operation. By the time he laid out his plans, the brothers were impressed. Hustlers themselves, they became interested in helping the kid.

Ebony watched curiously as her nephew was engrossed in deep conversation. When they left, Cam had a variety of merchandise that would at least triple his investment.

Business boomed! Cam had taken to posting up between the playground and candy lady, short stopping her sales. Some days between school and the complex Cam had to re-up twice.

On weekends Linda drove him over to Mr. Wright's store to his job. He not only swept the parking lot but absorbed every word his mentor uttered.

One thing Mr. Wright stressed was saving his money. Cam made sure to put away at least one third of his profits. Cam also watched how the local dealers who frequented the store operated. At six he saw that most of them were extremely careless. He watched them get knocked off at an incredible rate. They made it easy for the police.

When the school year ended Cam had to find something to replace the income loss. As he stood in line to meet with the Arabs, a plan formulated in his mind.

He watched droves of people buying bottled water and saw a hustle. Ali loaned him a Styrofoam cooler which he filled with frozen ice pops and bottled water.

Cam went to the basketball courts and sold out instantly. Kids couldn't wait hours between ice cream trucks so being 'Johnny on the spot" paid off.

Another young hustler also frequented the parks and courts. Tray was only in his early teens but had a booming weed business.

Quite a few times Tray and Cam shared bench space peddling their wares. Cam was impressed by the way he moved and studied him. He noticed that the majority of Tray's customers went to the store and bought cigars.

The Arabs frowned at selling him cigars until he explained himself. Impressed, they sold him boxes at cost allowing him to triple his money.

By middle school it was time for Cam to step his game up. He left his candy empire to Fernando and prepared to enter the big leagues.

"Say Shawty, put me on?" He demanded Tray.

"What you know about dis?" Tray laughed. He was amused until the kid spelled out his whole operation to him.

In truth Tray was ready to step up too. His business increased to where he was selling weight and dealing in exotic herbs like Purp, Kush, and Hydro.

However, there was still so much money to be made selling dimes of Reggie he couldn't just walk away. It's the curse of a hustler. It's hard to leave money on the table.

"Aight Shawty, tell ya what," Tray said sizing Cam up. "I'ma hit you off with a buck fifty a sack."

"Two fifty," Cam shot back instantly.

"Two," Try countered.

"Bet," Cam said extending his hand to seal the deal with a handshake. That was something Mr. Wright had taught him. It was now a lost art as there was no honor among thieves anymore. Eye contact and handshakes were out of style.

Cam figured that two bucks a sack should at least net him twenty bucks a day. That wasn't too bad. He figured wrong! He sold a hundred dime bags and took home two hundred dollars for the day. He was hooked. There was no turning back now.! Some days were better, others were worse but Cam took home at least a yard a day. His analytical mind searched for reasons for the increases and decreases in business. He ascertained that the first of the month and

31

Fridays were his best days. This allowed him to concentrate on the busy days and not waste time on the slow ones.

Since kids at school loved to smoke weed but most couldn't afford ten bucks, Cam hatched yet a new hustle. He invested in rolling paper and rolled up individual sticks for sale. Using two sheets of paper allowed him to roll six sticks per dime bag netting him an additional two bucks per.

CHAPTER

9

C am walked into Columbia High on his first day fresh to death. Whatever was hot he had it on, punctuated by a Braves hat on top and the latest Jordans on the bottom. He was sitting on plenty of money in his stash but he made sure he and Fernando stayed fresh.

He was re-united with his best friend Bobby. They stayed close over the years but this was the first time being in the same school since kindergarten. He also took notice of how fine Trish had gotten. She was a year and a grade ahead of them so she basically blew him off as a kid. However, once word got out that he was that dude, Trish took notice too.

Everyone took notice including Octavius. The old rivalry still existed, now fueled by jealousy. There was a tenuous truce that could be broken at any moment. Both knew it would one day be broken. It was only a matter of time.

It was also only of a matter of time until young Cam got himself some pussy. Girls flocked around because of his status as the weed man but he had yet to hit something – partly because he was in love with Trish. She may have dismissed him as a little brother, but to him she was his wife.

That all changed in an instant. Cam was a shrewd businessman and never extended any credit. Mr. Wright explained to him early on that it was bad business. If you it to give, then give it, but never give credit.

"Business is never personal," he explained to his protégée. "Shit is valuable when you want it but don't have it. Why you think hoes charge for pussy before you get it? Cuz it ain't worth a damn once you finished!"

"Hey Cam," Daffney sang sticking her head inside the basement door.

Daffney was the village whore. Eighteen, two kids and super fine. Ghetto fine – big titties, fat ass and never enough clothes on.

"What's good Shawty," Cam said without looking up from the video game.

"Shit smoke one!" Daffney announced plopping down beside him. When she did her breast bounced causing Cam to fumble the ball on the game.

He glanced at the short skirt and tank that showed all her smooth black skin. Cam had to swallow the lump in his throat before he could speak.

"You know I don't smoke no weed Shawty," Cam croaked.

"Well let me smoke one," she said sweetly placing her hand on his thigh. Her hand slid up and found him hard as a rock.

"Shit, take care of me, and I'll take care of this," she said squeezing his dick.

Cam watched anxiously as she rolled and smoked a blunt. When she finished she leaned back and lifted her skirt. She slid her panties to the side and let him slide inside of her.

After a good solid minute of humping Cam released inside of her.

"OK thanks," Daffney said pushing him off as soon as he bust a nut.

He was a little confused by her lack of emotion as she jumped up and walked away. Still he was elated by his first piece of ass and wanted to share the news. Fernando wasn't around to tell so he went over to see Tray.

"Just got me some pussy!" he announced as he walked in. He felt so good he wanted a parade or something.

"Who you hit? Daffney?" Tray replied nonchalantly.

"How you know?" Cam said feeling wounded.

"Shit, everybody fuck Daffney. She got some good, good!" Tray explained.

"You hit that too?" he pleaded.

"Shawty err body hit that! The mailman her baby daddy!" Tray laughed.

Still Cam fucked Daffney on a daily basis. Trish had his heart but wasn't checking for him. When Daffney's period came on she gave him his first blow job. He viewed her as practice and she taught him how to please a woman.

Cam's Grandma Linda threw Cam a party for his sixteenth birthday at the skating rink on Columbia Drive. It was off the hook!

Half the school was in attendance and half of Decatur. Cam took his lil cousin shopping at South DeKalb Mall, finally spending a little of that weed money.

Ebony had braided both their hair and they were fresh to death. Of course she overcharged Cam. Lately she kept her palm extended. She was changing. Cam had seen it before and it troubled him.

After sexing Daffney on a regular Cam was ready to spread his wings. All the attention he was getting at his party said tonight was the night.

"There go that duck Octavius," Bobby said pointing out his nemesis.

Cam nodded but didn't speak. Him and his special guests shared a large table. Guests came to wish him happy birthday. Some even bore gifts. Most bought weed from Bobby who was handling transactions for the night.

"Hey Cam," Sessalie sang. She didn't really sing the words but her beauty made them sound like a song. Her walk looked like a dance, and her smile could melt ice and hearts instantly.

"Hey yourself," Cam said seductively. He had his eye on the beauty queen from day one but never had the balls to approach her. Now that he had his weight up a little she approached him.

"Happy birthday. You want me to sit with y'all?" Sessalie asked as he'd possibly say no.

"He cool. Kick rocks!" Trish announced harshly.

Sessalie sucked her teeth and walked off. Trish chumped off the next few girls who came up as well.

"Say Shawty you can't be dissing all my people," Cam said sternly.

"Shit you can't be talking to no other bitches in my face!" Trish shot back angrily.

"Why not? You ain't my girl!" Cam shot back still not getting it.

"I ain't ya gurl?" Trish demanded. "So now I ain't yo gurl?"

"So if you my girl, then cut something," Cam told her in her ear.

Trish crossed her arms and balled up her face.

"That's what I thought," Cam said standing up.

"OK," Trish announced grabbing his shirt to prevent him from walking off.

"OK what," Cam demanded standing over her.

OK, I'ma do it," she said meekly.

"Say Nando, I finna bounce for a minute," Cam told his cousin as he led Trish from the rink.

Tray was out front sitting on his car kicking it with some young girls when Cam rushed out with Trish in tow.

The young girls were crazy about the custom Cutlass so when Cam selected one to take a ride she jumped at the chance.

Cam and Trish shared their first kisses as they traveled back to the apartment. Meanwhile Tray was trying to get the girl to go down on him along the ride. "Just kiss it, just the top."

Once at the house Cam took his time with her. Slowly undressing her, kissing skin as it became exposed. It shocked him how wet Trish was, then again how tight she was.

It wasn't until he pushed inside of her he realized she was a virgin. The young couple made love until Cameron couldn't take it any more. With a grunt he came in Trish and slumped on top of her.

"What's wrong?" Trish asked. "You done? Is it supposed to be that quick."

"Oh you got jokes," he laughed. "Lucky I spared your ass."

They joked, laughed, cuddled and kissed until Tray honked the horn. The couple quickly dressed and ran back to the car. Tray's young friend looked pissed so Trish asked what was wrong.

"This nasty bastard," the girl said, before spitting out the window again.

"What you did to her?" Trish demanded.

"Skeeted in her mouth," Tray laughed cracking Cam up as well.

The party was breaking up as they pulled back into the parking lot. Cam chuckled to himself when he saw Daffney jumping in a car full of dudes.

A commotion on the side of the parking lot caught all of their attention.

"Is Bobby Dem???" Trish yelled springing from the car.

Cam and Tray also got out and rushed towards the action. Bobby, Fernando and a few more guys from Eastwyck were hooking with Octavius and company from Glenwood. It was like that every weekend. Hoods fighting other hoods.

Belvadere vs. Scotdale, or Candle vs. Glenwood. Fernando was only 14 but tall for his age and loved to fight. He was handling his man pretty well but Cam still ran to help him. The two of them made quick work of dude.

Cam then turned his sights on Octavius who was trading punches with Tack from Eastwyck. He caught him from his blind side and dropped him. Him and Tack showed Octavius some fancy foot work while he was down.

"Twelve!" People began shouting as police cruisers pulled in from every angle. The kids all scrambled in different directions to avoid capture.

Trish and Fernando were already at Tray's car when Cam made it. He jumped in and chirped out away from the scene. Bobby and the rest followed in Tack's car.

"What happened Shawty?" Cam asked his cousin once they cleared the parking lot.

"That fuck nigga Octavius was trying me," Fernando fumed. "Slick hatin' poppin' shit bout you pushed from your own party cuz you saw him. Why you bounce anyway cuz?"

Cam and Trish shot each other a glance and smiled at the memory of their encounter.

"Then what happened?" Cam said changing the focus.

"Shit, I swung on the nigga! Fuck him," Fernando explained.

CHAPTER

10

C am bought the Cutlass off Tray for two stacks - rims, system and all. His grandmother was going to take him to get his license that weekend so until then he joy rided around the complex.

"Let's take a ride Shawty," Tray said sitting in his new Tahoe when Cam pulled up.

Cam accepted the blunt of purp when it was passed and took a light toke. It was his first time smoking. He was the lone holdout as the rest of his crew including Fernando all smoked weed by now.

"You doing it big lil Shawty," Tray complimented.

"A lil something," Cam said modestly. In fact under the circumstances he was doing quite well. He had his cousin selling weed in his school, Bobby had his apartments and he held down Eastwyck.

Even after forking over two grand for the car, he still had seven more stashed and a few hundred in his pocket. Unknown to most is that included in that seven grand was some candy money from first grade. Mr. Wright taught him well.

"Well it's time for you to move up," Tray announced.

He'd since started selling strictly premium and didn't have time to middle man all the pounds Cam and his crew was running through. Tray had been selling them pounds for a thousand, making a two hundred dollar profit.

After a right on McAfee Tray hung a few lefts and pulled into a driveway.

"This my man Slim. My connect," he said getting out of the car.

Cam followed him into the house to meet Slim. Slim stood 6'5" and may have weighed 180 with his keys in his pocket.

"Slim dis my lil nigga Cam," Tray said making the introductions.

"What it do Shawty?" Slim drawled extending a slender hand. "Tray say you dat dude."

"Coolin," Cam replied leaving the compliment in the air.

"Cam gone fuck with you direct," Tray said officially putting his student in the driver's seat.

"That's what's up," Slim agreed giving him a business card.

Cam fought not to frown at the card with a weed plant and his name and number. In his mind he thought, "this nigga is stupid."

"Come blaze up with me," Tray invited once they returned to Eastwyck.

"I gotta holla at my people real quick," Cam said jumping out the truck.

"OK fall through when you finished," Tray said going to his apartment.

When Cam got in, Trish called and kept him on the phone for hours. He finally managed to get free only to get into a conversation with his grandmother. After that Daffney came over offering a blow job to smoke a blunt.

Cam finally managed to get back over to Tray's apartment well after nightfall. He heard some shouting as he approached, then saw two flashes accompanied by gun shots. He wisely ducked between parked cars just as two men sprinted from the apartment.

His heart stopped as the men ran straight toward him both with guns in their hands. One had the duffle bag Tray used to transport his weed. The men got into the next car over from where Cam was hiding.

Cam knew the car and he knew the faces. It was Black and his brother Scoop. He saw them clearly as the vehicle's dome light illuminated. When they pulled off Cam rushed inside to check on his mentor.

Tray sat wide-eyed on the sofa with a neat bullet wound in the center of his head. Only a small trickle of blood leaked down his face. Another bloodier wound ruined his shirt.

Decatur was a jungle and like any jungle there are rules. Rules of the jungle dictate that no matter how close two lions may be, when one dies the other will eat him.

Cam went in his pocket and removed a large wad of cash. He sat it on the table as he was in search of something far more valuable. Cam fished out Tray's cell phone and shoved it in his own pocket.

He decided not to leave the cash for the police to steal and shoved that too in his pocket. See that's another rule of the jungle, first cop on the scene gets to keep whatever he finds. That's why you see police running lights, sirens, and flashing lights. First come, first served.

Cam took his place in the crowd as the police did their thing. He thought of his mother for the first time in years as he saw his mentor carried out in a body bag.

He felt no sorrow, just a slow boiling rage. His mind was made up instantly. Black and Scoop had to die. He had to kill them. He would kill them.

"That's some lame ass shit," Slim lamented when he let Cam in. It was only a day after the murder but the whole hood heard about it already. Wild rumors were tossed around but Cam kept his secret.

"Yeah, fucked up Shawty," Cam replied solemnly.

"What cha tryna cop?" Slim said passing a rather pungent smelling blunt to his guest.

"I need a couple elbows but I can only pay $700 for them," Cam said watching Slim's face. He knew Tray had been paying eight and charging them a stack.

"Shit Shawty I c...

"But I need ten!" Cam injected tossing seven thousand on the table.

The amount of cash overruled the slight short he was taking.

"That's what's up," Slim said greedily reaching for the money.

He disappeared to he back only to return a minute later with a bag. Slim pulled out 10 pounds of compressed weed handing them to their new owner.

"You got heat?" Slim asked with concern. "See how they did my boy."

"What a gun?" Cam asked as if the thought never crossed his mind.

"Shawty dese nigga's play the game raw! You better stay strapped," Slim urged.

"You got something?" Cam asked urgently.

Slim picked up a sofa cushion and passed his guest an old revolver.

Don't turn ya nose up at it," Slim laughed. "It may be ugly but she get the job done. Been putting niggas in the dirt for twenty years. This bitch hotter than that gurl Daffney in y'all 'partments."

"How much?" Cam asked, mesmerized by the sense of power the weapon gave him. It was almost sensual.

"Shit, gamma sixty," Slim offered. "I still got my bitch!" Slim produced an AK-47 assault rifle from behind the sofa.

"What you want for that?" Cam shouted fighting an erection.

"You ain't ready for dat!" Slim laughed putting the chopper away.

CHAPTER
11

Tray had a pretty good turn out at his funeral. The whole apartment complex showed up and half of Candler Road. Again, Cam flashed to his mom remembering her deserted funeral in this very church.

"Excuse me ma'am, but are you Tray's mama?" Cam asked a grieving woman in the front row.

"Yes, Tracey was my son," she said forcing a smile.

"I'm sorry," was all he could come up with as he dug in his pocket. "This was your son's money. He asked me to hold it."

"Thank you so much young man," she said sincerely. Many of her sons friends offered their condolences but nothing more.

Cam never counted the money nor entertained the thought of keeping it. He was living proof that real niggas did real things.

Cam almost choked when he saw Black and Scoop walk into the church. He couldn't believe their audacity to show up at the funeral they caused. He fought the urge to get his gun and lay them down on the spot.

Several people asked me who was taking over for Tray. Business still went on so Cam advised them to call Tray's same number. He was taking over for Tray himself.

By the time Cam reached Eastwyck and turned the phone on it was full of texts and voicemails. He spent the new few hours filling orders until his stock was depleted.

He went back to Slim for another ten pounds to fill the next days orders. Cam was officially in the big leagues.

"Would you look at this," Cam smiled to himself as he peeped Black pulling Sherita to the darkened basketball courts.

Sherita was a baby in a grown woman's body. At 14 she put must grown women to shame. She appeared to be resisting but the grown man wasn't taking no for an answer.

Cam rushed down to his apartment and packed. He walked the perimeter fence playing the wood line back to the courts. After slipping into the woods he crept up on his prey.

He was now a hunter. A lion easing through the tall grass. Inch by inch, stealthy step after step.

"Un uh nooo," Sherita whined, as Black tried to force himself on her.

"Shhh goddamn it," Black growled. He was s far gone he was going to rape the young girl.

He roughly pulled her panties to the side and was preparing to enter her as Cam emerged from the woods.

Sherita was pleading for her virginity when the slug from the 38 special lifted the would be rapist clean off her. Her and

Cam made brief eye contact before he slipped back into the woods and fled the murder scene.

Cam made it back to the apartment and into the basement. He still had the gun in hand as he sank into the sofa. The murder had him shook up, but at the same time, he liked it!

Fernando came down and saw his big cousin shaking like a leaf. He saw the gun in hand and went into action. He slipped the weapon out of his hand, wiping it down as he left through the back door. Since Eastwyck has a wooded area between it and I-20, he felt confident in tossing it away.

Once back inside Fernando lit a blunt and put it in his cousin's mouth. Wordlessly they smoked the weed until Cam was back.

"One down," Cam said with a smile, "one to go."

***

Life in the hood was a vicious cycle of life and death. Cam was awakened the next morning by his angry girlfriend standing over him.

"Wake up!" Trish demanded. We finna talk."

"Girl chill!" Cam said flipping over in an attempt to go back to sleep.

"Oh nigga you want sleep when you got my ass pregnant!" she snapped.

"Uh huh I know," Cam replied before her words actually set in.

"Uh huh! That's all you got to say," Trish yelled giving him a punch.

"Girl! What the hell you talking bout?" Cam said finally sitting up.

"I'm talking bout your ass getting me pregnant!" she said plopping down beside him.

"Pregnant?" He asked incredulously. "What you gone do?"

"Yes, pregnant. I'm bout to have a baby that's what!" she said before the tears began.

Neither kid wanted a kid at 16 but it was what it was. Life in the hood perpetuated itself.

CHAPTER
12

C am fought the move to cocaine for as long as he possibly could. His crew was begging to make the jump, but he was a fan of the late, great B.I.G. Cam new that mo money meant mo problems. Still he made the switch.

"A thousand dollars! For an ounce?" Cam exclaimed.

"Shit Shawty you gone make bout twenty five huned off it! Today!" Slim explained.

"Shit ain't moving like that," Cam replied dubiously. His crew had assured him it was, but he just couldn't see it.

Everybody smoked weed, everybody. He even smelled the aroma seeping from under his sweet grandmother's room a time or two. But crack! Was crack really moving like weed?

Slim showed Cam how to cook, cut and bag the dope. He quickly absorbed the lesson and would not have to be shown again. Cam was like that. In any other situation he could have soared to whatever heights he wanted. But he was in the hood, so he excelled at all things hood.

Since Bobby had been beggin for some work so much Cam made him his first stop. He gave him 125 of the 250 sacks he bagged off the ounce.

While there, he figured he may as well break Trish off with a little wood. The couple barely finished copulating when Bobby began banking at Trish's bedroom door.

"Say Shawty! Come out here!" he said almost hysterically.

Cam pulled his pants on and rushed to open the locked door.

"What's wrong Shawty!?" he said snatching the door open.

"Wrong? Dis look wrong to you!" Bobby replied thrusting a wad of cash in his face.

"Fuck is this?" Cam asked puzzled. No way he sold a half an ounce in half an hour.

"Shawty we done knocked that off! Gimme some more!" Bobby demanded.

Cam counted out twelve hundred and fifty dollars and smiled. He'd handed 250 back to Bobby along with the other half ounce. He whipped out his phone and hit his new best friend.

"I need to bump back into you Shawty," Cam said fighting to contain his enthusiasm.

"Told ya!" Slim laughed, "Come on through!"

"Perfect!" Slim congratulated Cam on cooking up his first batch.

He gave Cam 2.25 ounces (what we know as two and a quarter in the street) for 1900. Cam paid him the stack in his pocket and agreed to bring him the other nine shortly. As they spoke Bobby hit him to inform he was done and to 'bring more work'!

Cam dropped another ounce off with Bobby and took the rest to the 'Wyck'. He put Ant and Tack on agreeing to pay twenty bucks on the hundred.

"What about me Shawty," Fernando said almost whining. He wanted some of that quick and easy dope money too, but Cam wanted to protect his baby cousin from it.

Cam was no fool. He knew these new riches came at a price. He was prepared to pay it but not at the expense of family.

"Look Shawty, I'ma handle the blow, you gone take over the green," Cam said hoping to appease him. He didn't. Fernando agreed halfheartedly. He wanted in on the big money.

A few hours later Cam paid Slim $3,500.00 for his last 4.5 (4 ½) ounces. He saw right then that Slim's limited supply would ultimately limit him. He knew from day one he needed a new connect.

He also purchased a "slightly used" chrome 380 pistol, cause mo money, mo problems.

Cam only had a time to cook up one ounce at Slim's. He dropped that off to Bobby and headed home to cook the rest.

The apartment was quiet so Cam assumed everyone was asleep. He set up shop on the kitchen counter. The cocaine was already in the water when he heard footsteps descending the stairs.

Cam prayed it was only Fernando, but it was his nosy ass aunt. He tried in vain to stand in front of the stove and block her view.

"Don't try to hide it, I can smell it!" Ebony announced triumphantly.

"You smelt it from upstairs?" Cam questioned. He suspected she was smoking from her increasingly erratic behavior.

"Yep, I smelt it in my sleep!" she bragged. "Now break me off!"

"What you on dope now"! he said with disdain.

"I 'party' a lil. So what?" she shot back indignantly. Crackheads had a habit of getting mad at others cuz they smoke dope. "Now break me off or I'm telling!"

"Well you gotta wait!" Cam shot back. And he made her wait. Wait til it dried, was cut and bagged before breaking off two sacks.

"That's it!" she complained, "two sacks." He threw her two more that sent her rushing from the room. Cam glanced at her still fat ass jiggle as she bounced out the kitchen. Ebony was fine, but he wondered for how long, now that she was smoking.

"Bring me back three stacks," Cam told Bobby as he dropped him two more ounces.

That's what's up!" He exclaimed at the raise.

Ant and Tack were pumping in Eastwyck and by midday all the work was worked. Cam anxiously waited on Slim to hit him when he got on.

When the call finally came he rushed over and bought another 4.5 ounces. Cam thoroughly checked the house this time before beginning to cook. It was empty but as soon as the crack hit the water Ebony appeared.

"Fuck you came from? The closet?" Cam said pissed at the intrusion.

"Don't worry bout all dat! Break me off," she demanded.

Cam again made her wait until he finished before giving her a few sacks. Again she complained but Cam held firm. "That's it! Beat it!"

He saw Daffney roaming around when he hit his workers off. Rumor had it she was trimming around with the dope. Cam called her over and took her inside.

"What's up boo?" Daffney said as they took a seat on the living room sofa.

Cam tossed a sack of dope on the coffee table then leaned back and pulled out his dick. Daffney looked at the dope then the dick and took both.

She was working her neck furiously and didn't stop when Ebony cam back and sat down.

"Break me off."

"Hey girl," Daffney paused long enough to say.

"What's up girl, Cam break me off!" Ebony demanded.

"You see I'm busy!" He shot back grabbing Daffney's head for emphasis.

"I'll wait," she shot back and stayed while he got a blow job. She even complimented the girl on her technique offering a few pointers.

"Girl suck that dick! Nigga's don't like all that hand shit," Ebony instructed.

Daffney took the directions and swallowed a few more inches of wood. The result was Cam blowing his load in her hot mouth.

"See! Got nephew's toes curled up," Ebony laughed.

Cam threw his aunt a few more sacks and her and Daffney rushed up the stairs to get high.

CHAPTER

13

School was officially over! No, it wasn't summer but the crew was making far too much money to waste time in school. Cam was the only one who took any interest in learning anything.

He generally spent his time between dropping off dope and picking up money, reading. He loved all the books from G-Street Chronicles but his literary diet consisted of more than street books.

Cam read everything he could get his hands on, math, science, history, even religion, but by far his interest was business. He read books about Ted Turner, Rupert Murdoch, Martha Stewart and Bob Johnson. People called him a hustler but to him they were the ultimate hustlers.

His crew was moving at least a four way everyday. That meant six stacks in his pocket after paying his workers. They all could do more if not for Slim's weak supply. They desperately needed a good connect.

Trish was getting bigger by the day as her child grew inside of her. Fernando and Sherita finally hooked up. Her and Cam shared an awkward moment the first time they came face to face. She wordlessly thanked him and he gave tacit 'your welcome'.

Cam finally parted with some of that candy money and bought a nearly new Tahoe. He gave Fernando the Cutlass as a bribe to stay out the coke business. He accepted but still longed to join the rest of the crew.

Aunt Ebony was tripping. Slipping is more like it. She always had a hand out looking for a hand out. If she caught Cam cooking she begged a few sacks out of him. If Fernando was careless to leave any money, anywhere, she took it. Out of his pockets when he slept, if he slept.

Linda was stressing at watching yet another daughter throwing her life away. She had to install a dead bolt on her door to keep her trinkets from disappearing.

The kicker came when she offered her own nephew a blow job for dope. That's when Cam began to think things might be better if she wasn't around. It would be easier than to continue watching her die slowly… killing herself softly with hard.

Scoop must have thought the heat was off and had been spotted in the hood lately. He was wrong and as soon as Cam caught up with him he would be dead wrong.

✳✳✳

"Say Shawty, I'm up to the pool hall," Ant said just above a whisper.

"And?" Cam replied wondering why he called him to tell him that.

"Dat fuck nigga Scoop up in here," he replied.

"OK! Stay put. Keep an eye on him! Call me if he leave!" Cam rattled.

His plan was to walk and shoot Scoop in his head. Fuck a witness. As he prepared to leave, common sense prevailed and a better plan was formulated.

"Ebony," Cam called summoning his aunt to his room. "You wanna make some money?"

Ebony looked at her nephew in his boxers, and went to kneel before him.

"Not that!" he shouted pushing her away. "Go get dressed. Something nice."

He had to send her back to change three times before she got it right. The sexy shorts and tight tee had her looking like the hottie she once was. Even at 31, Ebony looked like twenty year old.

She saw Cam tuck a 40 caliber pistol in his pants but said nothing. They rode to the pool hall in complete silence until they arrived.

"Since you like to suck dick so much, I want you to hit my man off," Cam directed.

"Who?" Ebony asked eagerly. It didn't matter. She was above discriminating on whose dick she sucked at this point.

"Don't tell him I'm here, just get him back to the Wyck!" He demanded.

"If you shoot him got you gotta pay me extra!" Ebony demanded. She was no fool, she knew he planned to kill dude and didn't give a fuck as long as she got paid.

Cam watched as aunt turned heads when she entered he establishment. All the dudes shot at her but she only had eyes for Scoop.

They made small talk for a few minutes before Scoop 'talked' her into leaving. He watched anxiously as his aunt guided him back to Eastwyck.

She led him to the back of the complex and next to a dumpster as directed. Cam parked and crept around the long way.

Since this would be his last blow job, Ebony did her best. Scoop leaned his head back enjoying the back of her throat.

Cam could hear his aunt slurping loudly as he inched nearer. When he heard Scoop announce he was coming, Cam sent him away. He snatched the door open and pumped two quick rounds in his face. Without hesitation he put Ebony out of her misery with two more shots.

He was shook up after his murder but this time he felt nothing. Almost nothing that is. Seeing the blow job sent him to Daffney's after disposing of yet another murder weapon in the woods.

CHAPTER
14

C am couldn't understand why Fernando was so broken up over his mother's death. Didn't he know she was on the dope? Falling off.

He thought he would be relieved to have her out of her misery. To compensate Cam bought him an old bubble Chevy. It looked so good after the rims and paint, Cam bought himself one too.

Bobby copped one as well, followed by Tack and everyone even remotely connected to the crew. It was a sight to see when all those custom whips pulled into any set.

The whole crew got gold grills from Candler Road to go along with the chains, watches and rings. They were dubbed the B.C.B. crew which was short for the Bubble Chevy Boys.

Trish gave birth to their daughter Kayla and Cam put them in a nearby apartment complex. It was time to separate himself from the action. He ran his operation from the basement of Eastwyck still, but didn't sleep there.

At 17 they couldn't get into the real clubs so they hit all the teenage spots. Everywhere the B.C.'s went they got a lot of love and a lot of hate.

They made a scene when they came and again they left with the hottest girls. They wore the best clothes and smoked the finest herbs.

The clubs that catered to Atlanta's teen population could not serve alcohol but turned a blind eye to the packages their patrons smuggled in.

ERV-G was performing at the teen club on Gresham and half the city showed up. As usual the B.C. pulled in twenty deep all blasting his hit songs from his latest cd.

The girls openly sweated the crew trying to pick one. Of course the haters hated cuz that's what haters to. Especially one in particular.

Octavius and his little crew had their apartment on lock and were getting a little money, but they couldn't see Cam with a telescope the way he was taking off.

The two crews mean mugged each other from opposite sides of the small V.I.P. It was a powder keg of tension and the slightest spark could set it off.

Shay was just that spark. Lil mama stood five foot even but was toting around the ass of an Amazon. Her tits were also out of place on her otherwise small frame.

Her shoulder length hair was cut to perfectly frame her pretty face. The short, tight tube dress she wore showcased her talents to a 'T'!

That not what it did for Cam though. It was her eyes. He never seen a brown skin girl with blue eyes. He would have dismissed them as contacts until Ant assured him otherwise. At that point he had to have her.

Shay was a gold digger to her heart. She went where the money went, and was pretty enough to get in.

She came in and sat next to Octavius since she knew he was generous with his ill gotten gains. When she made eye contact with Cam she inwardly cursed her decision.

Cam wore no more jewelry than anyone on his team, less in fact, yet it was clear that he was in charge. His crew deferred to him like royalty and it impressed the young girl.

Octavius was spitting his best game in Shay's ear but she didn't hear one syllable. Her and Cam locked eyes and communicated nonverbally.

Without uttering one word Cam said, "I wanna fuck you," and she telepathically said, "OK, but you gotta spend money on me." "No problem, I got money."

Cam nodded and invited her over with his finger. Octavius was in mid-sentence when she got up and walked off. The dis would have been bad if you was on the moon and no one saw it, but in a club full of people! In front of ya boys! It was unforgivable.

Cam stood when Shay arrived and led her towards the door.

Had he looked back he would have seen Octavius and company get up and follow. Had they looked back they would have seen Fernando, Tack and the rest of the B.C.'s following them.

Cam just hit the alarm on his car when the melee erupted. He dropped his keys and ran to join the fray. The two groups engaged in an all out slug fest until po-po rolled up.

The county police jumped in the battle swinging their batons at the kids heads. They were as much thugs as the ones they arrested. The kids didn't just take it, they fought back.

Soon it was two groups against the cops. Cam heard a loud 'crack' followed by darkness. A baton shot ended the fight for him. He woke up briefly in the back of a patrol car then passed out again.

The next time he woke up he was being pulled from the car into the intake of the county jail. Still groggy from the blow, Cam was dragged through the intake process and placed alone in a cell.

The deputies separated the two crews as best they could, but when one of Octavius' boys kept running his mouth they tossed him in with the B.C.'s. When they pulled him out a minute later he was unconscious, naked and missing a tooth.

They separated all combatants on different sides and floors of the massive jail. Cam ended up on the 6th floor in Pod 500.

Since it was well past lock down, the dorm was quiet. Cam took his mat into the cell and tossed it on the top bunk. The occupant of the bottom stirred and looked up.

"Sup migo," Cam said cordially but got no reply.

The Mexican sucked his teeth and rolled over to go back to sleep.

"Fuck you too," Cam thought as he climbed into his rack. As soon as he drifted off to sleep, the doors popped for breakfast.

Cam watched the 30 something men line up on the stairs as a food cart was wheeled in. Since he was hungry he fell in at the back of the line.

He turned his nose up at the cold grits, hard bread and yellow substance the inmates called eggs. Unable to look at the food let alone eat, he gave it to a junky he knew from Eastwyck and went back to his cell.

"Hope I'm out dis bitch for I starve to death," he lamented.

"Yeah it's some bullshit!" His Mexican bunk mate replied. "You want a Honey Bun or something?"

The Mexican pulled storage bin from under his bunk that was filled to the brim with food items. He spoke more like one of the west coast Esse's then the variety they had around Atlanta.

"Yeah I'll take one of them buns. 'preciate that Migo, Cam said.

The Mexican's smile disappeared and he stared at Cam.

"What's wrong with you?" Cam shot, confused at the obvious attitude.

"That migo shit homie?" He shot back, "How you like to be called nigga?"

"Call me nigga and finna hook!" Cam explained squaring off.

64

"And! Call me migo again we gone hook!" The Mexican said standing his ground.

There was a brief stand off. Neither man really wanted that type of problem. Neither man was going to back down either.

"Cam!" Cameron offered roughly.

"Huh?" The Mexican asked, puzzled.

"That's my name. Cam," he replied.

"Diego," the man said extending his hand. "My name is Diego."

The men shook hands erasing the tension instantly. They sat down and tore into Honey Buns and snacks for breakfast.

"So what you in for Shawty? I mean Diego," Cam inquired.

"Shawty's worse than Migo!!" Diego laughed. " A bullshit weed charge! Can you believe that? As much Ya as I move, I get arrested for a blunt in an ashtray. And I don't even smoke!"

"Fucked up Shaw... uh Diego. How long we gotta stay up here," Cam asked unsure of the procedure.

"As soon as they get us across the street, the judge will give us bond and we out," Diego explained.

"So what you mean, about moving 'Ya'? You got that work? I got a sick lil crew but my connect is weak," Cam laid out.

"You? You look kinda young," Diego countered. "'Sides I was just talking. Reckless at that. I ain't doing nothing."

When the doors next unlocked everyone was forced into the day room. After calling home, Cam kicked it with some dudes he knew from the hood.

Diego seemed to ignore the other Mexicans in the dorm. Instead he spend every second on the phone. Cam watched him. He wasn't boo loving with some chick. He was talking business. He was giving orders, making moves.

After a beat up sandwich for lunch, the dorm was supposed to lock down again. When the phones were cut off, Diego went into the cell.

Cam noticed four young dudes from across town follow him in.

"They finna get that migo," one of Cam's associates said.

"Why?" Cam asked.

"Shit why not?" Another kid laughed.

Cam rushed into the room just as the first one swung on Diego. He ducked the weak hook and threw a semi pro combo that put the kid to sleep.

The other three rushed in and attacked. Cam pulled one off and floored him. That made an even two on two until a few more Blacks jumped and the Mexicans sat by and watched.

Luckily for Cam and Diego the guards saw the commotion and called a code. Officers swarmed in and broke it up before it got too bad. The two got a few lumps but came out OK.

Since they couldn't be left in the dorm, Cam and Diego had to be moved to another floor.

"I appreciate what you did back there," Diego said sincerely.

"Ain't nothing Shawty," Cam replied nonchalantly. He hated injustice just for the sake of injustice.

"No it is something!! Diego said triumphantly. Honor and respect was a big deal to him.

"You wanna thank me, let me get one of dem birds," Cam said trying his luck again. Everyone knows the Mexicans had all the work in Atlanta. If Diego didn't have it, he knew who did.

"You have a number?" Diego asked.

Cam gave him his cell number just before the guards came back to move them. He was taken up to the 7th floor but wouldn't be there long.

Just as he sat his mat down his name was called for court. A short, shackled walk later he was standing before a judge who gave him a $5,000.00 bond for obstruction of an officer.

As soon as the price was announced his faithful grandmother stood to go pay it. It still took another eight hours until Cam finally heard his name called to 'pack it up'.

Cam looked lustfully at the officer who was processing him out of the jail. She was a stallion with a chest that threatened to bust through her uniform. That tattoo of some dudes name on her neck said she was ghetto as hell.

He was open to spit a little game at her until he looked into the envelope that was supposed to contain his valuables.

"Say Shawty, where my money? And my chain?" Cam asked puzzled.

"That's everything," she announced nonchalantly.

"Fuck you talking bout bitch! I had two or three stacks and my chain!" Cam fumed.

"Bitch?" She questioned as if she wasn't familiar with the word.

They got into a heated argument until another officer cam to her aid. He threatened Cam with re-arrest if he didn't leave. For the first time in history, someone got kicked out of the jail!

***

"Hey you ain't see an older lady out here?" Cam asked the officer who was guarding the deserted waiting room.

The office shook his head for reply.

"How bout a young nigga wit golds?" He asked hoping Fernando was somewhere around.

That question too got a headshake for an answer. Cam shook his head and walked out front. He looked around curiously thinking no one was there to meet him.

As soon as the thought processed in his mind, his Chevy came into view.

"My nigga!" He exclaimed thinking his cousin came to scoop him. He thought wrong.

"Shay?" He said jumping into the car with the pretty girl behind the wheel.

"The one and only," she laughed pulling away from the curb. Shay handed Cam a tightly rolled blunt and pushed in the lighter.

"Where we going Shawty?" He replied when she drove past the entrance to 285, which was the way home.

"You'll see," she said seductively.

Cam nodded approvingly when she pulled into the parking lot of a nearby motel. They spent the rest of the night getting to know each other.

CHAPTER

15

C am was stressing! He had locked down his new apartment complex and a few others. All up and down Candler Road dudes were trying to get down with the B.C.'s.

His only problem was Slim's limited supply. He was trying to divide the four way he bought amongst all his workers but it just wasn't enough.

He almost ignored the private all on his phone; tired of people calling for drugs he couldn't sell them. Every time his phone rang he secretly prayed it would be Diego. This time it was.

"Sup Shawty," Diego laughed when Cam picked up.

"You migo!" Cam laughed back.

"I got your migo," Diego chuckled before getting down to business. "You got 17?"

"Shit I got 34!" Cam shot back no missing a beat.

"Food court. Lenox. One hour," Diego said hanging up before Cam could reply.

Cam pulled the thirty four thousand dollars from his stash and took off. He rolled alone but Fernando, Tack and Bobby strapped up and followed closely.

Diego was already seated in the food court enjoying lunch with a woman. He stood and exchanged pound with Cam before inviting him to sit.

Cam couldn't take his eyes off the exotic beauty Diego was with. She had jet black skin, straight hair, slanted eyes and didn't speak a word of English.

"She has a sister," Diego said breaking the trance.

"Huh?" Cam said as he snapped back into the present.

"I said she has a sister," he repeated. "Get your weight up and I'll introduce you.

"That's what's up," he agreed, hoping to one day take him up on the offer.

"You have that?" Diego asked.

Cam sat the bag of cash on the table. A nod from Diego set his woman in motion. She picked up he bag and walked to the restroom with Nando discretely following.

"Oh I see you brought muscle," Diego laughed at Fernando's amateur surveillance. He then pointed out Bobby staring from a few tables over, then Tack and Aunt playing the pay phones.

"No offense," Cam offered apologetically.

"None taken, smart move, this is not a game," Diego stressed. "I have twice as many you just don't see them.

71

A few minutes later the woman returned and smiled at Diego. The exchanged a few words in Spanish and a laugh.

"Let's walk," Diego said standing to leave. The woman grabbed her shopping bag and fell in step beside her man.

"Would you mind holding my bag?" The beautiful woman asked finally speaking English.

"Sure," Cam said eagerly as he accepted the bag.

"OK, call me when you need me again," Diego said extending his hand. It was then that Cam realized he was holding two kilos of coke.

They raced back to Decatur as quickly as posted speed limits let them. No sense getting a federal trafficking charge over a regular traffic ticket.

Cam was ready to set the block on fire. All of his workers from the spots sat by anxiously while he and Fernando cooked, cut and bagged the dope.

Even with a little weight Cam knew from experience that he could make more money selling dimes. For now that's all he would do and move up slowly.

In under a week he was sitting 75 grand strong! It was time to see Diego again. He peeped that Diego's girl took the cash and passed off the dope. Lesson learned. Diego's hands never got dirty and Cam vowed his wouldn't either.

Shay carried 68 thousand dollars in a shopping bag as they met Diego and his girl at 200 Atlanta. The women swapped bags as the men made small talk.

She put the coke in Fernando's back seat and he took off to go cook it. The two couples departed as cheerfully as they met.

The B.C.'s soon had every apartment complex on Candler Road on smash. From Flat Shoals to Memorial Drive was B.C. territory.

"Say Shawty we need to lock down dem hotels on Glenwood," Bobby suggested. "They getting money!"

"Too hot!" Cam said. "We straight where we at."

"Shit Shawty we missing hella money," Bobby stressed.

"Shawty we seeing plenty bread! Gotta let other niggas eat too," Cam replied bluntly.

He agreed halfheartedly which told Cam he was gonna do it anyway. When Bobby's sales picked up drastically he figured he made the move. Then a frantic phone call confirmed it.

"We got hit! We got hit!" Bobby yelled desperately.

"Slow down Shawty!" Cam yelled back, "Tell me what happened."

"The fuck nigga Octavius!" Bobby fumed. "Him and some nigga ran up in the room on us. They got me for four ounces and a couple of stacks.

"The money was in the room?" Cam asked scratching his head. Who keep dope and dough together? Where they do that at?

"He say he gone rob every spot you get," Bobby threw in, ignoring the question.

73

Cam heard that Octavius had a little robbing crew, bit if it was personal then he was gonna take it personal. Octavius would have to be dealt with. Soon.

CHAPTER

16

A month after hooking up with Diego, Cam was moving at least a key a day, everyday. He sold ounces and four ways to the mid-level dealers and still supplied his traps.

He bought Shay a new Honda Accord for her help. She was officially his chick on the side so it was no surprise when she came up pregnant.

Trish knew he fucked around and cared less about who with. She was wifey and she knew it. She held the keys to the castle which was Cam's heart. Her days were spent chillin, shopping or sexing her man. Whatever he wanted.

Diego and Cam were at the point where they didn't even meet anymore. Shay would take 170 grand to his girl once a week in exchange for ten kilos of pure cocaine.

One of Cam's ounce customers was an older cat named Charles. He was the owner of the strip club on Columbia Drive. The strip club sat next to a teen club that the crew used to frequent.

Cam longed to one day be granted entry into that strange new world. They used to watch the beautiful women come and go afraid to speak to them.

Charles was so thankful for the pure coke and good price, he invited Cam to the club. He accepted the offer and extended it to his whole team.

Armed with $5,000.00 in cash and three ounces Cam set out to treat his family.

"Pick one," Charles told the group as they passed the club. The group settled in and began to party. Cam, Nando, Bobby, and Tack were escorted to an elevated V.I.P. section with tinted glass.

More dancers came in to entertain the V.I.P.s. Cam was more interested in seeing his team enjoying themselves. He watched as they smoked, drank and made it rain. They were making him rich!

The door flew open and in walked a light skinned dancer who snatched everyone's attention away from whatever they were just doing. She scanned the room and quickly ascertained that Cam was the leader.

Her ass shifted from side to side as she walked and her heavy breasts bounced with each step.

"You must be Cam," she said with a husky voice topped by a New York accent.

"Yeah, and who are you?" Cam replied casually even though she ha his heart racing.

"I'm Precious, you want a dance?" She half asked, half demanded.

"Nah, I'm cool," Cam said regaining his composure. "Sit and chill," he ordered, making sure it sounded like an order.

When she complied, he gave her a bill loaded with coke and she dove in. In between snorts she told him all about herself.

Precious was actually named Precious. She was born and raised in the Bronx's notorious Highbridge section. She was 24 and in law school.

Cam wondered why a law student would be dancing in a strip club, but the way she devoured the coke answered him.

"Come on!" Precious said jumping and leading Cam from the room.

They entered a small room next door and sat on the leather sofa. Precious wasted no time stripping Cam naked. She began kissing his toes and sucking each one before moving up.

By the time she reached his knees Cam was wide open. "Come Shawty," he said trying to get inside her mouth.

"Chill son, I got this," Precious said pushing his head away.

When she did reach his dick he almost lost it when her tongue flicked across its head. Finally she took him deep in her head until she gagged. She locked eyes with Cam as she slowly sucked him off.

Precious wasn't finished yet. After swallowing everything he offered, she kept on until he was hard again, then rolled a rubber down on him. She turned around with her ass facing him and slid down on his dick.

Cam was breathless watching her perfect ass slide up and down on him. She began to pick up the pace as a puddle formed under her. She braced herself by placing her hands on his knees and began splashing with every stroke.

It was too much for Cam. He was so used to fucking young girls around the way, this grown woman was turning him out. When Precious yelled that she was coming, he came with her.

They smoked a blunt naked and basked in the after sex glow. When they finally dressed, Cam gave her $500.00 and his number. He then went back to catch up with his crew.

The V.I.P. was empty except for Bobby and the club's lone white girl. She was blowing him and didn't even look up when Cam entered the room.

Everyone else got their rocks off and rushed back to block to get their rocks off. The crew went back to work, money over bitches for real!

Cam lit another blunt as he walked over to the room's tinted glass. He surveyed the room and almost choked.

"Say Shawty look!" He exclaimed.

Bobby waddled over with his pants at his ankles, dick bobbing in the air. The shit would have been funny any other time but Cam had murder on his mind.

"Tell me if that's who I think it," Cam half whispered, pointing towards the bar.

"Dat's dat fuck nigga," Bobby agreed still bobbing. "Let's get his ass."

"Chill," Cam cautioned. "Not in here. We gone wait on them to leave."

"So I got a minute?" Bobby asked eagerly.

"Huh? I guess," Cam said never blinking from his target.

Bobby rushed back over to the white girl and flipped her over. He pushed inside of her and pounded himself to a quick nut. This time Cam did laugh.

When Octavius and his unlucky companion left the club, Cam was right behind him. They pulled off oblivious to the imminent danger tailing them. A few turns later they parked in front of a house on DelMonico Drive. Cam parked at the corner and watched. He waited to see if they were going into the house or were gonna make it easy for him. A flash of a lighter lighting a blunt said they were gonna make it easy for them.

"Here we go," Cam said chambering a round. "I got Octavius, you hit the driver."

Bobby didn't respond so Cam repeated himself. "I said you hit the driver, I got Octavius!" He demanded.

Bobby swallowed hard and nodded his head nervously. They crept, guns drawn toward the sitting ducks. They crouched directly behind the car and Cam rechecked his weapon.

"Let's go," he mouthed sending the murder in motion. They rushed up to each side of the car guns high.

Cam tapped on the glass with the gun so Octavius could see his face. He wanted him to know where he was going and who sent him.

Octavius attempted to say something–what, the world will never know cuz Cam's 40 cal blew his brains on the driver. The driver reached for his gun and raised it while Bobby watched.

Cam was confused at how this could be since he was supposed to be dead. Without time to analyze, Cam pumped a few slugs at his head and ended the threat.

He sprinted back to the car but Bobby beat him there. When they got in Bobby sat behind the wheel shaking like a leaf.

"Drive nigga!" Cam screamed, eager to flee the murder scene. "Let's get the fuck out of here!"

Bobby snapped out of it and put the car in gear. He hit Glenwood, then Candler and pulled into the complex adjacent to Eastwyck where Cam lived with his sister and niece.

Cam stormed inside with Bobby close on his heels.

"Say Shawty what the fuck was that!" Cam demanded. "Why you ain't bust!"

"I...I...froze...Shawty...I froze up," Bobby admitted. "The gun was so loud!"

"You almost got me killed!" Cam shouted.

"What's wrong?" Trish asked coming from the back.

"Nothing, go back to bed," Cam barked.

She looked at her brother, then back to her man before retreating to the rear of the apartment.

"Just give me your gun so I can get rid of them," Cam said calming back down.

"I don't got it," Bobby mumbled. "I dropped it."

"Dropped it?" Cam replied puzzled. "Dropped it where?"

"At the car...when you shot dem. It fell out my hand," Bobby said. "It was so loud!"

"Get out," Cam growled. He fought the urge to take him somewhere and shoot him too.

"What my brother did?" Trish asked when Cam finally came to the room.

"Ain't nothing," he replied still fuming.

She stood up to help him out of his clothes.

"Hmmp! Smell like pussy," Trish quipped.

"Pussy?" Cam laughed. "That's not pussy, I was sweating."

"So break me off then," she demanded. "If you ain't been fucking, then let me get some.

Cam was surprised he had anything left after Precious, but his body responded to his girl's touch. She looked at him oddly when he directed her to mount him backwards.

He held her hips and forced her to rough ride him just like Precious had just done. She came loudly and slumped off to the side.

"Whew! She said breathlessly. "What...ever...one of...dem hoes taught you...that! Tell her I said thank you!"

CHAPTER

17

By the time Cam was 21, he was officially 'that dude'. He had houses all over town. There was the large home on the west side he put his grandmother in. then the even larger one he and Trish lived in. They had another child and another on the way.

Shay was pregnant again too. She was still at home with her mother but Cam promised her a house too once she had the baby. He had Precious staying in the condo he bought downtown. She'd since finished law school but had yet to take the bar exam.

Life as a kept woman, or personal freak served her better. Cam gave her all the blow she wanted since she lived at his stash spot. In return she fucked and sucked him every time he turned the doorknob.

Diego was still the crew's connect but he still wouldn't budge on the ticket. He still taxed Cam for 17 stacks, no matter how many he bought.

Precious' brother Bo-Bo was major in New York and offering a better deal. He would let them go for 15 if he bought 10 or better, and the quality was just as good.

Cam was tempted but loyalty was too important. He go rich with Diego. Everyone was eating and no one got knocked. Something had to give.

***

"Hey Shawty what's up with that pack?" tack asked when Cam picked up.

Even though they switched pre-paid phones weekly, he still hated to talk business of any sort by phone.

"Shoulda been there," he replied in the disguised voice he reserved for pre-paid. His voice would never be recognizable on anybody's wire.

"That's what I'm saying," Tack said. He was in the apartment in Eastwyck which was still used to cook, cut and bag dope.

Cam gave Shay $170,000 to meet with Diego's girl. They still made all transactions for their men. Shay picked up dope and dropped it off in the Wyck. Cam wisely didn't go anywhere near the place. Months would pass where he didn't even see any blow. He only handled the money.

He dialed Shay and a strange woman answered. She kept asking 'who is this', so Cam hung up. His next call went to Diego's pre-paid but that went straight to voicemail.

Diego's personal line also went to voicemail and some advice he gave echoed in his mind. Diego once told Cam that you never go against your gut. If something don't feel right it wasn't.

"Dump the phones." He texted urgently to all the phones. His next call went to the landline at Eastwyck.

"Clean the house! Everybody out," he demanded to Ant when he picked up. Cam tossed his phone out the window and headed to his condo.

Ever the multi-tasker Cam watched the news, monitored a police scanner and surfed the next on his tablet while Precious gave him head.

He expected the worse and got it. One of the top stories for the day was a major cocaine bust. Since the police scanners were mute, it had to be the feds.

It was reported that over a hundred keys of coke was seized along with millions of dollars. Not to mention the guns and cars.

"Fuck!" Cam spat as Diego's face splashed on the screen.

"What?" Precious said, pausing the blow job.

"Nothing," he said pushing her head back down.

It got worse as Diego's girl's picture flashed followed by Shay's, followed by a bunch of Mexicans.

***

When Cam got to Shay's house he was met at the door by her little sister Britney. Perhaps little sister isn't the best way to describe her because she was thicker and taller than Shay already, at 16.

"Oh Cam!" she cried throwing her firm young body against his.

Even in this time of distress, Cam felt his body react to the girls touch. Luckily his and Shay's son rushed to his daddy.

Cam broke off the embrace and scooped up his son. Shay's mother walked in rather calmly given the situation. She was an older version of her daughters. Even now, in her late 30s she looked like a 22 year old.

"Well, as you know they got Shay," Mrs. Thompson said matter of factly.

"Feds?" Cam asked looking for confirmation t what he already suspected.

"Yeah, feds. Those Mexicans were big league. Shay was in the wrong place at the wrong time," she replied.

"What she charged with," he said holding his breath for her reply.

"Well, there's the illegal possession of legal currency for starters," Mrs. Thompson sighed.

"What?" Cam exclaimed at the mention of the oxymoronic term.

"I know," she laughed. "In this great country of ours, it's a crime to carry over $10,000.00 in cash, and I assume she had a bit more than 10 grand"?

"A bit," Cam agreed.

"Then given the nature of the arrest, they will probably give her a conspiracy charge," she explained.

"Well if she get bond pay it through the lawyer," Cam said.

Mrs. Thompson twisted her lips as if to say 'no shit'. She was a vet of he dope game. Shay and Britney's father ran this city in his day. She knew the business better than Cam.

Ultimately, shay was charged as a conspirator. Not just for attempt to possess, but in Diego's whole operation. She was on tape so many times they knew she was in deep. For that reason the judge denied bail even though she was pregnant.

The feds had everyone's number from Shay's phone but every time they called either some kid answered or a junky. They had nothing but Shay.

CHAPTER

18

With Diego out of the picture, Cam needed a new connect. Having no other options he told Precious to call her brother.

Bo-Bo was already at the condo with Precious when Cam arrived.

"What's good son," he said a hundred miles a minute.

"Chillin Shawty," Cam replied, giving him a pound. Cam gave him a quick once over when he stood.

He took note that the man was low key, plain jeans and shirt on top of Tim boots. A glance at the platinum chain and titanium watch were the only indicators that he didn't work for the county.

"My sister tells me you ready to shop wit a nigga?" Bo-Bo said.

"Perhaps, perhaps," Cam said non-commitedly. "If the price and product right we may can do something."

"The ticket is for 10 or better, and as for the product, you tell me," he said tossing an ounce of coke on the coffee table.

Cam picked up the bag and marveled at its content. It was darker than Diego's and flashed with different colors. It was almost pink.

"That's fish scale poppi," Bo-Bo laughed as Cam was obviously impressed.

"See what dis hit like," Cam said attempting to hand the bag to Precious.

"What? Hit like?" Precious said indignantly, catching Cam off balance. "You know I don't fuck with no blow," she said desperately.

"Yeah OK," Cam chuckled catching on that she didn't want her brother to know she was a coke head. But judging by the dubious expression on Bo-Bo's face he didn't buy the performance.

"Ayo P, go roll up," Bo said tossing his sister a sack of florescent green weed.

Once she was out of earshot they confirmed their first deal. Cam learned a new lesson, called 'need to know'. Since Precious didn't 'need to know' the details of the transaction, she wasn't privileged to hear. And that was his own sister.

Over a blunt of the most potent weed Cam had ever smoked, he and Bo-Bo became fast friends. Besides he different accents and slang, the two dope boys had a lot in common.

They kicked it about music, weed, bitches, clothes and of course the cocaine business. Cam was large but Bo-Bo was next level. He mentioned trips to places Cam never heard of.

Designers and cars he didn't know existed. Then of course back to cocaine.

"What's your whip game like 'B'?" Bo-Bo asked when the topic came to cooking up. It had been a minute since Cam actually did the cooking and he told him so.

"Ayo this fish scale ain't no joke," Bo-Bo announced. "Come on let me show you something.

Cam was amazed to see Bo 'whip' the ounce into two. He just doubled his money, just like that!

Cam counted out $150,000.00 and arranged pick up the next day.

"There she is right there," Cam told Fernando when he spotted the woman with the red hat. She was standing in the pick up lane at the airport.

Fernando pulled over and let the girl in. She swapped her bag for the identical one Cam brought as they circled around the concourse. When they returned to the spot they picked up, she got out and went on her way. Done deal!

"You catch all that?" Cam asked his cousin.

"Yeah! Nothing to it," Fernando replied.

"Good cuz from now on it's on you!" Cam said.

***

Cam felt a twinge of guilt when Shay's name flashed on his caller ID. It had been several months and he hadn't spoke with her at all. She knew not to call him from lock up and knew that he couldn't come visit.

He assumed it was her mother needing money for the lawyer again.

"Hey Miss Thompson," Cam said cheerfully upon answering.

"Hey baby it's me!" The voice sang.

"Shay?" He questioned and looked at the display again. "You home?"

"Yep and I..." Shay began.

"Hold up! I'm on the way," he blurted eager to get off the line.

Cam was a bundle of nerves as he made his way up Flat Shoals Parkway to the good part of Decatur where Shay's mother stayed. He looked at the driver of every car to see if it was a fed.

He even parked a mile away at the supermarket and walked the rest of the way.

"Hey baby!" Shay sang as Cam walked into the back door.

Britney just frowned up as the couple shared a wet kiss.

"My lawyer sa...," Shay began before Cam cut her off again.

"Let's talk in your room," he said leading her upstairs.

"Take your clothes off," Cam demanded as soon as they hit the bedroom.

"Oooh! I see somebody missed me," Shay cooed seductively as she came out of her clothes.

Cam wasn't in the mood for love though. He wanted to make sure the feds didn't put a wire on her. She stood naked with her pregnant belly between them.

He almost told her to get dressed since he was satisfied she wasn't wired. But when she got on the bed on her hands and knees aiming her coochie at him he had to touch it.

When he did, it got wet instantly soaking his fingers. Cam dropped his pants and pushed inside of her. He had to go easy since she was in her last trimester.

Cam almost stopped when he saw the bedroom door ease open. When he saw Britney peek in he smiled. Since she wanted a show, he stepped back a little and slowly long stroked Shay for her sister.

The combination of Shay's good pussy and Britney watching was too much. Cam pulled out and skeeted on her ass. Britney blew him a kiss before easing the door closed again. "Mmm, that was good daddy," Shay moaned.

He got a wash cloth and cleaned them both off and got dressed. Shay began to cry silently as she lay her head on his lap.

"Baby that place was horrible," Shay sobbed. "I missed you and Lil Cam."

"It's over with baby, you home now," Cam comforted, stroking he hair.

"They want me to give somebody up," she said just above a whisper. "If I don't I'ma go to prison.

"Who?" Cam pleaded trying to hide his growing anger. "Did they ask you about me?"

"No, they know I wasn't with them Mexicans. They wanna know who I was working for," she whined.

"What you tell 'em?" Cam said as his hand tightened around her hair.

"I ain't tell them nothing!" Shay said pulling his hand away. "They told me I have until I go back to court in three months or I'ma do five years! At least.

"Don't be no snitch," Cam stated plainly. "You tell, someone may try to hurt you!"

"You think so?" she asked fearfully, not knowing the someone he was talking about was himself.

"Yeah or me. You wouldn't want nobody to hurt me would you?" he said trying another approach.

"Noooo!" Shay said at the thought.

"Look baby, if you did have to go away you know you and your mom and Britney will be OK. Plus I'ma buy you a house, whatever kind of car you want and give you a hundred grand! Just don't be no snitch."

"OK baby. OK," Shay said unconvincingly and Cam was not convinced.

CHAPTER
19

Cam kept his word and spent a quarter mil on a large house for Shay. She moved her mother and sister in to keep her company in the large home.

She was still complaining about having to go to jail, but when she delivered their daughter Shanay, Cam knew she changed her mind.

Shay occasionally threw out names of crew members who she felt were expendable. Cam knew that is one of them fell, he was next.

"What' this for? Oh I love it!" Shay gushed when Cam had a designer dress delivered to her. "This the one I showed you at Lenox."

"That's for our honeymoon Shay. We getting married!" Cam exclaimed.

"For real? You serious? Don't play!" Shay screamed into the phone.

"Course I'm serious," Cam replied. "Now meet me downtown and let's celebrate!"

"I'ma leave right now!" Shay said eagerly.

"That's what's up," Cam said. "Hey do me a favor on your way?"

"Anything for you daddy!" she sang.

"OK, stop at the A-1 on Glenwood, Nando broke down," he said.

✷✷✷

Shay smiled when she saw Fernando at the gas station. He was standing next to his donk with the hood up. She planned to tease him about the old car. No matter how much money he crew made, Nando was addicted to old cars.

"Mmm hmp," Shay said through the passenger window as she pulled up. As soon as she stepped a foot out of the car 'Weasel' stepped away from the pay phone.

He lifted a 9 millimeter to the back of her head and squeezed off two shots. Shay was dead before she hit he ground.

Weasel jumped in her car and took off leaving her twitching on the ground. There were enough witnesses to the carjacking to squash all suspicion of a hit.

The car was chopped later that night and would never be seen again. Neither would Weasel, since Cam personally killed him.

"Fuck you do that for," Nando griped when Cam shot Weasel from behind.

"Why? I'll give you two reasons," Cam said seriously. "First off this nigga can't never snitch down the road, and second this nigga killed my baby momma!"

✳✳✳

Cam looked down at Shay in her casket. She did look great in that new dress she wanted so much.

"I'm sorry babe," he whispered feeling a bit of remorse. Still it was him or her as far as he was concerned. She knew the risk, and reaped plenty of the rewards.

"Oh Cam!" Ms. Thompson said when cam approached her on the front pew. She embraced him pressing her soft body tightly against him.

They rocked back and forth in their grief until Cam got an erection. She pulled back enough to look in his face. He was embarrassed at the improper reaction and walked off.

✳✳✳

It was another month before Cam went to see his kids again. The kids looked so much like their mother it troubled him.

He was relieved to see Ms. Thompson's car gone when he pulled into the driveway. Britney pulled the door open and ran into his arms.

"Oh Cam! Where you been?" she demanded.

"Where's Cam?" he asked looking at his baby daughter sleeping on the sofa.

"He went with momma, you just missed them," she replied.

Cam tried to ignore how fine she was in her cheerleaders outfit. She saw him checking her out and giggled appreciation.

"Smoke a blunt with me Cam," Britney pleaded.

"Girl you too young to be smoking," Cam chuckled.

"Boy stop! I'ma be 18 next week, I'm grown," she shot back. "I'm finna take Shanay upstairs."

Cam watched the short skirt rise up and show her perfectly round ass in blue spandex. He retrieved a blunt from his car just as Britney returned.

They smoked a blunt as she rambled on endlessly about stuff Cam could care less about. He didn't know who any of the rappers or singers she went on and on about. "D-Lite this and D-Lite that!"

"Wanna see our new routine?" Britney sang springing to her feet. Without waiting for him to reply she launched into a cheer.

Cam only half watched until Britney made a move that showed she had removed her shorts. She saw he noticed and gave him a show.

"Well? You like?" she said standing directly over him.

For a reply he pulled her skirt up and kissed her thighs. He laid her on the sofa and continued kissing her firm legs.

CHAPTER

20

"**B**oy, y'all shit one hundred lately," Charles exclaimed when Cam walked into his office. A lot of his customers had been singing the praises of his new product. As they spoke a police siren could be heard coming through the club's speakers.

"Fuck is that," Cam said feeling antsy at the unnerving sound.

"Oh that's Missy. She's a cop so she like to come on stage to that," Charles explained.

"A real cop? Dancing!" he replied astounded.

"Well, she work at the jail so I guess she police," he answered. Go check her out, she can go!"

Cam shook hands with Charles and headed up to the private V.I.P. to observe the show. The D.J. threw on a club banger by Erv-G and out came Missy.

She had a hat, holster and billy club along with her requisite bra and thong. Cam leaned up to get a better view of the familiar face. He knew he knew her but didn't know from where.

He pressed the intercom button that summoned a waitress and he studied Missy.

"Yeah sugar," the waitress said when she arrived.

"Say Shawty, let me get a bottle of champagne and send Missy up the second she step foot off that stage," he said punctuating the demand with a crisp hundred.

As soon as Missy walked into the V.I.P. he saw the tattoo on her neck and that reminded him of where he knew her from.

"You work to the jail Shawty!" he exclaimed as it came back to him. She was the officer he argued with when his cash and jewelry came up missing.

"Everybody know that, " Missy snapped. "Y'all gone get me fired, y'all keep running ya mouths."

"Your secret safe with me," Cam chuckled and lit a blunt of Kush. "Let me get a dance Ms. Officer."

"It's $50.00 a song in the V.I.P.," she cautioned as if he couldn't afford it.

"Dance!" He ordered peeling off a hundred dollar bill.

"What the county don't pay good enough?" Cam asked, only half watching her performance.

"They straight, I just be needing extra money, cuz I like to party," she explained.

When she said 'party' she subconsciously rubbed her nose. It was a telltale sign of someone using cocaine. He knew it all too well watching Bobby do it lately.

As Bobby popped in his mind, he pulled out his phone to hit him.

"I ain't boring you am I?" Missy quipped sarcastically

"Shit for fifty bucks a song you shouldn't give a fuck if I fell asleep up in this bitch," Cam laughed. "I know that's right," Missy laughed.

"Say Shawty, shoot me a half up here at Charles," Cam ordered when Bobby picked up.

"Must be a freak!" Bobby laughed. "I'ma tell my sister."

Cam wondered if he was gonna tell Trish he was getting high and fucking up packages and money while he was at it.

"I'ma send Lil D at cha," Bobby replied when Cam didn't.

It took 30 minutes and ten dances at $50.00 bucks a pop before Lil D arrived with the coke. He was out $500.00 already and planned to spend more. Having someone inside the jail would be priceless!

He shot Lil D a C-note for his pocket and sent him on his way. Missy watched him curiously as he dumped some of the pretty white powder on the small table in front of him.

She knew from his swag he didn't use, and assumed it was for her. Missy knelt in front of the table prepared to dive into the cocaine.

"Not so fast! First things first!" Cam announced before she could hit a line. When he had her attention, he leaned back and pulled his dick out.

"Nigga you got me fucked up!" Missy said indignantly. "I'm 'posed to suck your dick for some blow? Nigga I get plenty bread."

"First off," Cam began smoothly, "you ain't gone blow me for no blow cuz I ain't no trick!"

The statement almost made him laugh remembering how much money he spent tricking off in this same room over the years.

"You gone suck my dick cuz 'you' want to," he reasoned. "Then you gone snort some of that powder cuz 'you' want to! Then you gone take a little money for ya pocket cuz 'you' want to."

When Missy didn't respond Cam knew he had her.

"So, what do 'you' want to do?" Cam said leaning back again. He didn't understand her reply cuz his dick was in her mouth.

Missy, A.K.A. Officer Milton was now officially a member of the B.C.s. Putting her on the team paid off sooner than he thought.

✳✳✳

"Bobby on the phone!" Trish repeated shaking Cam.

"Tell him call back! Cam demanded before rolling back over attempting to go back to sleep.

"He said he in jail!" she said desperately.

"Jail! And he called our house?" Cam said shielding his eyes from the sunlight streaming into the room.

102

Cam snatched the phone from Trish's hand and stared at it for a second.

"Yeah!" he barked gruffly using the voice reserved for prepaid phones. He was hot about the breach of protocol, but now wasn't the time to talk about it.

"Shawty, I got knocked off on Glenwood," Bobby replied.

"Sorry to hear that," Cam said quickly. "How bad?"

"Shit, a quarter and toast," he replied sounding remorseful. And he should. Nine ounces of crack and a gun was a serious charge.

Again Cam wondered why Bobby carried a gun. He wasn't gonna bust nothing. Dude wasn't built for this shit. Nigga's love to floss and ball out, fuck the dope boy groupies and such, but half were soft.

"Aight, keep ya head up," Cam spat before hanging up the phone.

"Tell ya Momma to get him once they set him a bail. Tell her to use the house. No cash!" Cam told his girl.

Cam rushed out and wisely cleaned up everything Bobby was involved in. It would cost him tens of thousands of dollars, but Bobby was weak. He knew he couldn't be trusted.

When he returned home he found Trish in the living room sobbing.

"What's wrong Shawty?" he asked sitting beside her to comfort her.

"They was supposed to let Bobby get a bond. Then they charged him with a double murder!" she said crying.

He kept saying he sorry, "Tell Cam I said I'm sorry!" Trish whined.

That feeling of dread that proceeds danger overwhelmed Cameron. He looked at his front door just in time to watch it as it came off it's hinges.

"Search warrant!!!" The first of what had to be an army of police screamed as he rushed in. A flash bang grenade stunned the stunned couple and they hit the floor.

The first officers quickly and roughly secured Cam and Trish tightly in plastic cuffs. The small army fanned out throughout the house, guns first.

Shouts of 'clear', could be heard all over the house as the police secured room after room. Thankfully the children were at their grandmother's house.

Once the house was cleared the team began their futile search for drugs and weapons. Neither would be found, unless they brought them themselves.

Trish was released but Cam was carted off to jail. As soon as he was processed in they took him to be interviewed by homicide detectives. He was charged with the murders of Octavius and his driver.

They left him alone in a cold interview room for a couple hours hoping to psych him out.

"Lawyer!" Cam announced as soon as the door swung open.

"I haven't even said anything," the first cop in chuckled.

"Lawyer," Cam repeated. "Ain't nothing to say."

They attempted to question him for the next couple of hours. All they got out of him was "lawyer!"

He was taken back to the jail and housed on the 7th floor with the rest of the killers. Cam was treated like royalty when he entered the dorm.

His partner Q from Eastwyck kicked his bunkmate out of the cell so am could move in. Even gave up the coveted bottom bunk,

Just as he got settled in his name was called for an attorney visit. Q was impressed that his lawyer came so quickly, but if he knew how much he was paying him he would have realized he was only getting his money's worth.

George Stein was one of the best criminal lawyers in the state of Georgia. He had never lost at trial and won't even talk to you for less than $25 grand. Since this was a double homicide the ticket would be 50 stacks.

The men were separated by a thick glass partition and had to talk via closed telephone. He began to explain the details of what Cam had already figured out.

"Well, they have a witness," Mr. Stein said plainly. "If he testifies they will convict you."

Mr. Stein hung up the phone and stood. He looked at Cam to see if he understood. Cam nodded in agreement. Stein had just killed Bobby. It was almost as if he pulled the trigger himself. No witness, no case.

CHAPTER

21

"Cameron Forrest," the familiar voice called over the P.A. system. Cam stirred awake as his door was popped open.

"You're wanted in medical," the voice announced.

When he got into the hallway he stifled a smile. There was Missy twirling a set of handcuffs seductively.

"Turn around," she ordered suppressing a smile of her own.

She led him through the security door to the elevator. They waited in silence not even looking at each other. When the car came Officer Milton shoved her prisoner against the wall and shoved her tongue in his mouth. When she felt an erection rise in his uniform she reached down and stroked it. Once the elevator reached the third floor she rushed him into a supply closet and gave him a blow job.

"Mmm thanks officer. I needed that," Cam said on the way back to the elevator.

"No problem," Missy laughed. "You know ole boy left tonight on a signature bond."

"He signed his own bond on two bodies!" Cam exclaimed.

"You already know," she sighed. As the car neared the seventh floor she slipped a small cell phone and batter in his socks. "Nando 'posed to bring me some green for you so hold tight."

Cam nodded in appreciation. When he got back to his cell Q was awake.

"You straight Shawty?" he asked concerned about the unusual call out. Usually that meant you're a snitch.

"Super straight," he laughed before laying out the encounter.

Cam tried out the new phone and alerted Fernando to Bobby's release.

"I'm finna knock dis nigga block off!" Nando fumed.

"Nah, chill Shawty," Cam directed. "It's too soon. Just act like everything cool. Put the nigga back to work and everything."

"Dis nigga police!" his cousin griped.

"So you run the show now?" Cam barked to put the world back in perspective.

"You da man," Fernando said with a hint of sarcasm. "Tell me what to do then."

"Just chill. Get some purp to Missy so a nigga smoke a blunt up in this bitch," Cam said easing up.

The cousins made small talk for a few minutes before hanging up.

"Say Shawty I can take care of that for you," Q advised.

Cam listened as Qadar laid out the perfect plan. Q's murder game was the stuff of legend. It was well known that if Q was on your ass, life was short.

Still, he was only in on a probation violation since all the witnesses in his last case either died or caught amnesia.

"Chill Shawty. I'm sit for a minute," Cam advised. He knew it would shine the light back on him if something happened too quick. Better Bobby get back in the streets. The streets were dangerous. Anything could happen at any given time.

Cam planned to sit for a couple of months to deflect attention from him when the inevitable happened. But after three days he was super stressed.

The fake wannabe gangstas he shared space with threatened to drive him crazy. The outrageous lies they told at first amused him the pissed him off.

First all the killers! Cats running around the dorm bragging about all the niggas they killed. Cam had at least ten bodies under his belt and he never once bragged about it.

Then all the kingpins. What most of the liars didn't know is that they were bragging to the same man they indirectly got their work from. Silly niggas was tell him they were him!

Cam and Q never ate the trays when they came. Missy and her crew of insiders made sure he got whatever he wanted. He ate and smoked like he was home.

Trish brought the kids to see him when visiting day rolled around. She let the kids tell on each other for a few minutes before taking the phone.

"Your other kids downstairs," she said plainly.

"Say what?" Cam said genuinely confused by the statement.

"You and Shay kids," she replied. "Who dat, her sister?"

"You know about that?" Cam asked shocked.

"Been knew. I ain't tripping though," Trish shrugged.

Cam resolved right then to marry her, and told her so.

"It's bout time I marry you huh?" he laughed.

"As much shit I take you just ought to," she laughed.

When the thirty minutes came to a close Cam blew kisses with his kids as they left. The guard told him to stay put since his next visitors were on the way up.

A few moments later in walked Britney and his other kids. Lil Cam ran up to the glass and called for his father. Shanay smiled at the sight of her daddy.

As soon as Britney picked up the phone she bust into tears.

"Fuck wrong with you?" Cam asked curiously.

"I don't want to lose you!" she whined. "They said you got murder charges."

It took Cam a few minutes to calm her down. He assured her he would be OK, cuz he didn't even know what was going on.

"Guess what?" Britney gushed, grinning from ear to ear.

"What?" Cam chuckled not knowing where to begin to guess what had the young girl so happy.

"My period ain't come," she said proudly. "I'm finna have your baby."

Cam could only laugh and shake his head.

"What next?" he thought as they exited the visiting area.

Precious was next. Before Cam made the short walk to the dorm his name was called again. He turned and headed back. When he reached the top of the stairs, Precious had come through the door.

"What's good Ma?" he teased in his mock New York accent. He and Bo-Bo had grown close over the last few months.

Bo was super protective of his sister so Cam kept her around, no matter how much she got on his nerves.

"I need some blow!" she demanded as soon s she picked up the phone.

"Blow? Are you crazy?" Cam said astounded. "Fuck you talking about blow! On these recorded phones!"

"My bad daddy," Precious said sincerely, "I just need you. When you coming home?"

"No idea!" Cam lied. He knew full well he would be out soon, but since that date coincided with Bobby's murder it was best not to say.

"Let me see something," he said seductively, to change the subject.

"You like?" Precious sang standing up to show off her outfit.

She lifted the short skirt as Cam directed and masturbated for him. Since he knew his visit would be replayed he gave them something to listen to.

After three weeks Cam couldn't wait anymore and gave Q the nod. Bobby was directed to Atlanta's west side to drop off half a block of cocaine.

He didn't know it was payment for his own murder. Qadar's brother Ramel executed Bobby as soon as he arrived. The gun in the car along with the bags of crack ensured the murder would be treated as drug related. Drug related in Atlanta meant swept under the rug.

Trish knew not to call Cam's cell phone unless it was life or death. When Cam saw the number he knew it was death.

"They killed my brother!" she wailed. "Bobby's dead."

"Slow down! Now what happened?" Cam said pretending to be hearing the good news for the first time.

He was glad she couldn't see the big smile on is face as he spoke. "Who?" he demanded as if he planned to straighten it.

"I'll be home in a minute," he assured her since the only witness against him was now a corpse.

As soon as the news broke about Bobby's death, Mr. Stein was at the D.A.'s office. They still wouldn't concede but Cameron was given a $25,000.00 cash bond.

Cam left the cell phone and weed to Q when he left and promised him a new job. Bobby's old one.

CHAPTER

22

C am stepped out of the musty jail and into the fresh night air. He inhaled deeply in an attempt to clear any residue of the stale recycled air from his lungs. He looked around wondering who Fernando sent to pick him up.

He frowned when a spankin new Masarati flashed its lights and whipped up to the curb.

"I know he ain't send nobody up here in a fuckin Masarati," Cam cursed at the foolishness. He shook his head when he saw who was driving.

"You don't think this is a bit much for the jail?" Cam asked bluntly.

"Fuck the police," Nando laughed. "My shit all legal!"

"You reckless cuz," Cam warned before switching gears. "What's up with the import? Thought you were a donk for life nigga."

"Shit, I got so much extra dough since I put my team in Kirkwood," Fernando bragged.

"Kirkwood! Nigga the feds just knocked off the whole block! And you put a team in there!" Cam exploded. "We discussed that shit and I told you no! Fuckin feds still there cleaning shit up."

"Nigga you said 'you' ain't wanna go down there," Fernando explained. "So I put 'my own' shit down there.

"Yo shit?" What, so you the boss now," Cam shot back.

"Nah you 'the' boss, but I'm 'a boss'," he replied arrogantly.

"Whatever," Cam sighed slumping back into the Italian leather.

Again he thought seriously about quitting. He had plenty of money, and was growing tired of the drama. What they don't show you in the movies is the toll murder takes on the killer. Yes killers have feelings too.

His lawyer had over two million of his money in various banks. He was set for life. All he had to do was let go. That was the hard part.

"Where to my nigga?" Fernando asked his weary cousin.

"Home, Trish home," he specified. "We got a wedding and a funeral to plan."

A few days after the funeral Cam swung out to see his other kids. Britney jumped up and down when he pulled up. She was loading the kids into car seats preparing to leave.

"Cam!" she sang rushing over to hug him.

"Bad timing I see," Cam said. "I'll come back later."

"No cuz my mom wanna talk to you," she said.

"Your mom? Bout what?" he asked curiously.

"She gave me a test. I'm pregnant! For sure!" she said bouncing with excitement. She lifted her tight shirt and patted her hard belly as if she were showing.

Cam peeled her off a few hundreds and went inside to face Ms. Thompson. When he didn't find her anywhere downstairs, he called upstairs.

"Up here," Ms. Thompson's sweet voice rang through the house. "In here."

"Oh! My bad!" Cam apologized when he entered her bedroom.

She had just gotten out of the shower and was wrapped in towel.. Barely.

"Yeah right!" she laughed at his attempted humility. "I see how you look at me. Don't act shy now."

Cam watched in awe as she slowly, seductively applied lotion to her thick caramel legs. He mouth dropped when the towel dropped.

"Boy done knocked both my daughters up!" she chuckled, shaking her head.

Cam tried to speak up, but was waved off by Ms. Thompson.

"Britney started getting a pissy little attitude lately so I knew she must have got her some dick. Girls are like that. Then she started running around 'Cam this, Cam that'. It

115

reminded me f how Shay was when she first met you. You must got it going on."

"I really don't know what to tell you," Cam admitted sheepishly.

"Ain't nothing to tell," she said climbing on her huge bed. "You may as well go for the trifecta."

"Excuse me?" he questioned as she lay back and spread her legs.

"Hope you know how to eat pussy," she replied wickedly.

He did! Boy did he. Cam ate his baby mother's mother until she screamed, shook, and shivered.

Then he flipped her over and gave he just what she wanted. They ran through every sexual scenario until honked the horn in the driveway.

"Guess you best go help with the bags," Ms. Thompson said casually. "We gotta set up a schedule mister."

"Cam was exhausted. Not just physically but mentally. He needed a break, a getaway. He scanned his contact list in his phone looking for escape.

"That's what's up!" he announced halfway through the Bs.

"Damn son! I know you ain't ready again. We just dropped off yesterday," Bo-Bo exclaimed.

"Nah dis personal Shawty. A nigga need a break," Cam explained.

"Word, word, just say when nigga," he replied.

116

"Now!" Cam laughed. "I'm on my way to the airport now!"

CHAPTER

23

"When the next flight to New York?" Cam asked staring up at the flight schedule.

"We have a flight to JFK boarding in 30 minutes and hum!" The ticket clerk paused to check availability. "Yes there are seats available.

Cam absent mindedly removed a large wad of cash from his pocket. He missed the clerk's reaction to his bankroll. They were taught to report transactions just like this.

Last minute flights, no luggage, cash, spelled one thing, drug dealer.Cam's name was entered into a database along with pictures of the transaction.

He called Trish to alert her of his impending absence as he made is way to the gate. It dawned on him that for all his money this was his first flight. His first trip outside of his state. His trip outside of the metro area.

Most first time flyers feel some anxiety about flying, but not Cam. He was sleep before the plane taxied to the runway. He had to be awakened once the plane landed in New York.

Bo scooped him in a spanking new Bentley GT and headed the opposite direction of the bright city lights.

"You ain't bring no bags yo?" Bo-Bo asked breaking the silence.

"Nah Shawty, I figure I'll cop some gear while up here," he replied.

"That's a beet. I'll take you shopping in the morning," he said.

Precious had often spoke about how nice Bo's house was but Cam still wasn't prepared for what he was seeing.

The Bentley glided around a circular driveway in front of a mansion. The house was worthy of MTV cribs.

Cam wondered if Bo was having a party when he saw all the cars in the driveway.

"Got company huh?" he asked as they pulled into a parking space.

"Huh? Naw these mine," Bo-Bo replied nonchalantly.

They parked between a fairly new Lamborghini and brand new Rolls Royce. They walked past an Austin Martin, Range Ruff Porche, Humma and a couple of cars Cam never seen before.

The inside of the house was an exact replica of Tony Montana's, complete with fountain.

"Look familiar?" Bo asked with a laugh.

"Fuckin scar face!" Cam exclaimed. "This shit is sick!"

He led Cam into the den with it's 100" flat screen and huge sectional sofa.

"So what you tryna get into?" Bo-Bo- asked reaching for bowl of weed. The huge crystal bowl contained the fluffiest, prettiest weed he ever saw. It looked like lime green popcorn.

"Wanna hit a club, or eat, or I can order some pussy if you want," Bo offered.

"No pussy!" Cam laughed thinking about his recent romp with Ms. Thompson.

"Precious putting it on you like that!" Bo laughed. "You taking care of my sister?"

Cam wanted to tell him his sister was a cokehead and he was past ready to dump her.

"She's good," he said instead. In the end they ended staying in talking business over blunts and beer. Cam stayed in one of the house's guest suites.

In the morning Bo took Cam to get some new clothes. First they stopped in the nearby town of Wyandanch, New York.

He was amazed at how quickly and drastically the scenery had changed. Dix Hills may be a short drive but it's a world away from the 'danch'.

Cam couldn't help but notice how much Wyandanch looked like Decatur as they passed junkies and trappers lined up on its main street.

The town was technically in the suburbs but hood at the same time. That's a feat only niggas can achieve. Bo was treated like a head of state when he parked the super charged Range Rover.

"What's this?" Cam inquired wondering why they were here.

"Home," Bo replied. "This is where I grew up. Now I own it.

"What, this shop?" Cam said as they entered the barbershop.

"The block," Bo said triumphantly. "And the next one too. Oh and the supermarket, taxi company, and Chinese restaurant.

After a cut, the men headed toward New York City.

"Yo 'B' we finna hit Jamaica Avenue," Cam said mixing his slang.

"Naw Shawty," Bo laughed. The Avenue is for small timers. "Real Ballers don't shop on the avenue.

Their first stop was at the Gucci store, then Prada and the other high end stores in the clothing district.

Bo put Cam on a new style. For the first time in his life he bought slacks and sweaters. Purses and shoes for Trish and Precious. He picked out watches and subdued jewelry at the high end stores.

Cam's money was no good the whole day. His host spent thousands on him showing him his city. Cam vowed to extend the same courtesy next time he came south.

When they returned to the Long Island Mansion, Bo had company. His cousin Chris Barnes and childhood friend Easy were in the den.

"Yo cuz this is Cam, Cam this is Chris," Bo said making the introduction.

"Bout time," Chris chuckled. He had been doing most the drops but never met Cam. He and Nando met once a week.

"For sure," Cam said giving the man a pound. "Heard a lot about you."

"In fact he had heard a lot about the killer from the Bronx. Chris, although a pretty boy, was a stone cold killer. He was the muscle of the operation bar none.

Precious told him once back when they were teenagers some knucklehead made the mistake of slapping her. Chris chased the dude for blocks shooting at him. The dude ran up in the 41st Precinct thinking he was safe, but Chris came in behind him. He killed him right at the front desk. The police were so stunned, Chris was gone before they could react. Now that's gangsta!

The men went to the indoor pool where 15 of the world's baddest women waited. Waited topless. There were a couple of East Indian girls, black, white, Asian and Latino.

"See anything you like?" Bo laughed at his guest's shocked look.

Chris wasted no time. He led a pretty Spanish girl to a lounge chair and laid back. When he pulled out the wood she went to work.

Easy followed suit, except with two girls. Cam grabbed the Indian girl and he and Bo just got a massage and smoked a blunt.

After a week on the strange planet Cam headed home. Again, at the airport, he paid cash for the next flight. He paid twice as much for all his luggage than for the last minute flight.

The alert clerk attempted to report the irregularity but Cam was already flagged. The entry of his name set off silent alarms from New York to Atlanta.

"Excuse me," a black suited man said as Cam pulled the last of his bags from the conveyer. "Can we have a word with you?"

Cam shrugged his shoulders as the agents picked up his bags. He knew he was clean so he wasn't concerned. They took him to a large room where other agents waited.

One of the agents was a drop dead gorgeous black girl. She and Cam locked eyes and shared a discrete smile. He didn't hear most of what they said to him for looking at the beauty. Not to mention he didn't care.

"Looks like we got a bootlegger," one agent announced as he opened the large duffle bag filled with designer purses and shoes.

The black girl made a beeline to inspect the merchandise. She checked each one shaking her head as she did.

"They're all real, all of them!" she said not bothering to hide her excitement.

Cam watched as the men searched his clothes, even tallying up the still attached price tags. As they did, the female agent went through his cell phone pressing way more buttons than necessary.

"Sixty thousand!" the red faced agent exclaimed staring at the calculator.

"Sixteen in cash," another announced after tallying up the cash from his pocket.

"Y'all finished, can I go now?" Cam finally asked growing frustrated.

"Yeah you're free to go," the agent in charge smiled. "But um... we'll 'catch' you later."

Cam thanked his luck that he drove his SUV to the airport instead of a two seater as he loaded all the luggage. He paid the long term parking and hit the highway. He didn't get too far before his phone vibrated in his pocket. He frowned at the unfamiliar name on the display. "Who the fuck is Demi?" he asked no one.

"Yeah!" Cam barked upon answering the phone.

"Sixty thousand! On clothes?" Agent Demitrice Jones laughed.

"You know, somehow I figured it was you," Cam smiled. "Knew your ass was feeling a young nigga."

"Be that as it may, this is a business call," Demi said professionally.

"You calling my personal number makes it personal," Cam replied.

"Well I got student loans out my pretty ass so it's my personal business," she shot back.

"So how can I help you then?" he asked.

"Actually, it's how I can help you," Demi corrected, "and it'll only cost you fifty."

"Where, when?"

CHAPTER

24

"Well what do you think?" Mr. Stein smiled as he pulled up. They were meeting at the building Cam was looking to buy. Bo had convinced him to invest his money into legitimate ventures so he was planning on opening a club.

His lawyer talked him into buying a whole building instead of leasing. They set up a shell corporation to legalize the dope money. Besides the couple mil Stein had offshore for Cam, this venture was costing a few million more. This was tying up all his cash.

Cam was serious about moving away from the drugs. He even looked legit since cutting his braids and trading baggy jeans for custom slacks and loafers.

After viewing the property, Cam agreed to the deal, sending Stein in motion. They shook hands and separated to their next meetings. Stein went to the bank to arrange financing.

Cam had an engagement at a hotel near the airport. He used the stairs and knocked on the 4th floor suite.

"Good timing!" Demi said pulling the door open. "I love a man who comes, on time."

"Thought you said business," Cam said frowning.

"I love a man who gets down to business too," the agent nodded.

"Well, here I am, here is the fifty," Cam said tossing a paper sack on the bed. "What's the biz?"

"That was a stupid move moving into Kirkwood before we even left," she said plainly.

"Shows how much you know," Cam chuckled. "That ain't even me.

"Of course not. You're far too smart for that. We know Fernando made that move on his own," Demi said.

"So the fifty saves my cousin?" he asked eagerly.

"Oh no!" she shook her head animatedly. "He's done! We let him sell fifty or sixty keys. He's beyond help."

"So what the fuck am I giving you fifty stacks for," Cam demanded.

"First you paid for the info I just gave you. Tell your cousin to run! Go on the run cuz he's done. Next, it's a down payment on me," she replied.

"You?" Cam asked puzzled. "So I'm buying pussy now?"

"You haven't made enough to buy this pussy!" Demi laughed. "They haven't printed enough money to buy my body. But I am assigned to you. You are my caseload. This fifty plus twenty a month means we never get nothing on you."

"You ain't got nothing on me anyway!" Cam said picking his money off the bed.

"No?" Demi questioned. She handed him pictures of him and Bo all over New York. Cam sat the bag back down and listened.

***

"Ball 'til you fall Shawty!" Fernando laughed. "It's pat of the game Shawty!"

"Game? Is that what you think this shit is? A game?" Cam exclaimed.

He couldn't believe how stupid his cousin was. After alerting him to his impending bust the arrogant fucker wouldn't listen.

"Shawty you outa touch!" Nando shot back. "Look at you cuz! You got on loafers! I'm in dem streets Shawty. I'm the dude now! I been meeting Chris getting my own packages for months.

"You the dude?" Cam questioned getting hot. "I'm outa touch? Me?"

"Yeah nigga," Fernando laughed. "I'm the king now! Dope Boy fo life!"

Cam watched his foolish cousin leave. He tried. There was nothing else he could do.

CHAPTER

25

A gent Demi was worth every penny of the monthly fee. Because of her, Cam's name was excluded from three separate investigations. Even with the feds up Bo's ass, he was still able to re-up without being seen.

Fernando was a few kilos away from a life sentence. Cam reached out to him a few more times with the same result.

Meanwhile Cam moved full steam ahead with his club. He was hands on wanting to be involved in every aspect. He selected the system, the paint, even the liquor. This was his entrance into legitimacy.

He was interviewing prospective waiters and waitresses when 'Demi' appeared on his phone.

"Agent," he said curtly, indicative of their love/hate relationship.

"Look, you know our business is business but you need to check on your condo," she said and hung up.

Cam wrapped up and took the short drive up Peachtree Street to his condo. When he walked in the first thing he saw was Precious and some guy.

They were both butt naked on the sofa. Cam wasn't sure what pissed him off more, the bare asses on his sofa or the block of his coke they were indulging in.

"Both of y'all get up and get out my shit!" Cam demanded.

Bo would just have to understand, cuz it was time for Precious to go. Her services as personal freak were no longer needed. Now she's in his stash.

"Hold up nigga!" the dude said grabbing Cam's wrist when he reached for his coke.

Cam wasted no time in stomping the naked man to sleep. Precious jumped on his back and tried to claw his eyes. He spun her off and knocked her out with an upper cut.

He opened the door and dragged the sleeping couple to the curb. Cam quickly gathered up Precious' possessions and left them at the curb with them before heading back to the club.

After getting the DJ and bartenders straight, Cam had some family obligations to tend to. Britney had given birth so he headed out to see his new son.

"There go your daddy," Britney sang as Cam walked into her room.

Cam took his son and smiled. He couldn't help but notice how much he looked like Lil Cam. And with the same father and two sisters as mothers why wouldn't he.

Tired from the days events Cam wound up in bed with mother and child. He awoke in the middle of the night and headed to the kitchen. He was drinking juice from the carton when Ms. Thompson appeared.

"You know you dead wrong," she whispered seductively.

Cam took in the sexy gown and knew she was right. He should have been back to hit her.

"I'm here now," he said putting the carton back.

Ms. Thompson led him into the living room and bent over the sofa. Cam lifted up her gown and rammed into her. There was no foreplay, no tenderness. He pounded her savagely causing her knees to buckle as she came.

"Oh no you don't," Cam chuckled as she began to melt. He grabbed her waist and slammed himself in and out of her. He actually growled when he came inside of her.

She chuckled as he slumped onto her back. "You OK youngin? Tried to fuck me and you the one can't stand up."

"You know you love this dick," Cam said pulling out of her.

"Mmm I do!" she exclaimed. "But you gotta stop coming in me. I ain't too old to get pregnant. You got kids by both my daughters! I ain't tryna be on Springer!"

***

The next morning when Cam got in his car he saw that Bo had been calling all night. He knew he would be hot about his sister, but still business was business. They were making millions. He'd get over it.

He disregarded the voicemails and called Bo direct.

"Ayo B you hit my sister!" Bo said so fast it took Cam's mind a second to catch up.

"It wasn't even all that," Cam tried to reason even as the memory of the beating flashed back. He stifled a chuckle at the thought. Precious had been begging to get her ass whipped for months, years even.

"Just tell me if you hit my sister! You touched my sister nigga!" Bo shot back.

"Be easy Shawty, I know we ain't finna fall out bout no bitch!" Cam frowned.

"Bitch? You calling my family out they name," he asked.

Bo-Bo was talking so fast it was comical, and he laughed. The more he tried to control it the harder it got. Finally he had to pull over and drop the phone to get it all out.

"Shit funny!" Bo screamed. "You think the shit funny Bitch nigga!"

"OK, OK, my bad," Cam said still chuckling. "Look Shawty, we getting too much money to go out over some bitch! Any bitch. Fuck dat junky bitch!"

"Fuck her? That's what you said" Fuck my sister?" Bo raged. Son was out of control. "You a dead man!"

The line went dead and both men dialed separate calls.

"Who, where and when?" Q asked ready to murder anybody, anywhere, any time.

"New York ass niggas, soon, they coming," Cam replied. What he didn't know is that 'they' were already here.

Bo's call went to his cousin Chris who just so happened to be riding with Fernando. They were swapping dope for dough when the shit hit the fan.

"Sho nuff?" Chris laughed when Bo declared war. "Shit I'm with Nando now. OK that's what's up.

"Who dat?" Fernando replied at the mention of his name.

"Ain't nothing," Chris replied. "Say pull over real quick."

As soon as Fernando pulled his car to a stop Chris shot him twice in the side of his head. He reached over and pulled the door handle letting the corpse fall out. He slid over sitting on blood and brain matter as he pulled off. A glance at the body made him smile but the bag containing 300,000 grand made him smile harder.

CHAPTER

26

When Cam saw Sherita's name on his phone's display he pressed ignore sending the call to his voicemail. Her call alone told him all he needed to know. Fernando was dead.

He'd been trying to reach him frantically ever since Bo threatened him. Nando's body had just been identified at the morgue.

The next move was Cam's so he had Q kidnap Precious from the club. They lured her out with a big bag of coke on to her death. It would not be a quick easy death.

Precious was taken to an empty house where she was raped, tortured, and beaten in front of a video camera. Q made sure to make her blame her brother for her death before he took her whole face off with shotgun blast.

When Bo got the video he blew Cam's condo up. That shook Cam up. The blast was so big it took out the units on both sides killing the occupants.

Cam was a killer, but Bo-Bo was a terrorist. Who blows up a whole building? He wisely ducked out of sight until he could figure out what to do.

He took Trish and the kids to the mountain house no one knew about. Q and his goons staked out Bo's long island mansion, but he went underground as well.

It was a standoff. Until the call came.

"Lucky Lady, Miami Beach, sails in two days," the voice said before hanging up.

Two days was just enough time for Cam and company to drive down to Miami. By the time Bo-Bo, Chris and the harem of exotic beauties boarded they were already in place.

Demi gleamed from her co-workers that Bo was taking a mil in cash to the Bahamas. For twenty percent, she made the call.

Since no one knew Q and his two hired guns, they took the place of the paid off crew. Meanwhile Cam was crouched in a closet watching the action.

The hit squad communicated via text message on muted phones. When the boat reached open water it was time.

"Excuse me ladies," Q said politely waving a 40 cal pistol. "Please follow the gentleman with the MP-5 on deck."

"Who the fuck is you?" Chris demanded. He was strapped and ready to go out blazing.

"Chill 'B'," Bo spoke up. "Where yo man at?"

"Right here," Cam said extricating himself from the cramped crawl space. "Check mate nigga!"

"Check mate? Or just check?" Bo smiled

Chris was tense, ready to rock.

"If you here then you know what's in the duffle bag," Bo reasoned.

"Yep," Cam smiled, "my money."

"Come on B, we can't go out like this!" Chris snarled. He could care less about the guns pointed at him. If he was gonna die then it would be going for his gun.

"Breath easy son, we can work this out," Bo cautioned. As he spoke he inched closer to his own gun. When Q's man came back in he created the split second both men needed to pull.

Both Q and Cam focused on Chris which allowed Bo to come up shooting. His first round caught Q's goon in the eye spraying the wall when it came out.

Chris took off shooting wildly as he ran. Q and Bo traded shots with each other until they were both mortally wounded. Even as they lay on the ground dying they tried to reload. Neither of them made it.

Cam chased Chris dumping as he ran. Chris didn't even slow down when he hit the deck and ran straight into the ocean.

When the firing stopped Cam was the last man standing. He directed the captain to return to shore. Cam paid off the captain and made the long drive to Atlanta lone, which is how he planned to return anyway.

Q was his dude but he planned to go legit. The last thing he needed was old bodies coming back to haunt him. The consolation was not having to kill Q himself.

After Demi's 200 grand, Cam still had plenty of cash. He dropped a hundred on the club and book another buck with him to Vegas.

After all she'd been through, it was time for him to marry Trish. Chicks like her are rare. They scream 'ride or die' but they don't mean it.

Trish has been down since day one. She put up with all the bullshit, all the bitches, and stayed down.

They had a quick ceremony in a cheap chapel, then went and blew 50 grand shooting craps. The newlyweds spent a week in Sin City returning just in time for the big opening.

CHAPTER

27

With all the money Cameron pumped into the club it was sure to pay off. It was the newest trend in a trendy city. It was also a novel idea of catering to more than one genre.

There were actually three mini-clubs. The main floor played all the latest hits spun by the city's best DJs.

Downstairs played hip hop and reggae which attracted another segment of ATL partygoers. Each had a separate entrance, although staff could pass freely.

The open air rooftop was dedicated to quiet storm type R&B or Jazz. Tonight a band did dead on renditions of Sade's biggest hits.

"You did it!" Trish gushed proudly at her husband.

"We, did it," he corrected extending his glass for a toast.

The patio level was filling up just as the other levels were. A line around the block meant some partygoers would have a long wait while others wouldn't get in.

"The gentleman sent this," one of the waitresses said sitting a bottle of champagne on the table.

"Who?" Cam smiled scanning the room to thank the donor.

He squinted dangerously at the face behind the raised glass. "Can't be!" he thought, but it was! And thinking instead of ducking was not a good look.

Cam dove across the table to take his wife to the ground just as the shots rang out. The gunfire came from a male, female team sitting behind Trish.

Chris got up and walked out casually as the shooting began. Trish grunted loudly as a heavy slug slammed into her back. When it ripped through her heart she died instantly.

The rent a cop rushed over and traded shots with the team. He too went down dropping his gun as he rushed off to meet his maker.

Cam scooped up the gun taking cover behind the fallen cop. He peeked up once sending a volley of shots at the dead man.

The next time he peeked up he sent shots. A well placed round caught the woman in the center of her forehead. Her partner panicked and began shooting wildly as he ran.

Cam took off after him returning fire. A round to the buttocks slowed the man down dramatically. He caught up with him in the middle of the street in front of the hundreds standing in line.

In full view of all the partygoers and off duty but uniformed police, Cam executed the man. The first head shot killed him, the next two were just to make Cam feel better.

He laid the empty weapon in the street as ordered by the police. It wasn't until he attempted to raise his hands above his head that he realized he'd been hit.

An ambulance took him to Grady Memorial where he waited for hours to have the bullet removed from his shoulder. After surgery Cam was escorted to the Fulton Jail and for the second time in his life charged with double homicide.

✳✳✳

Luckily for Cam a judge dropped the charges to one count of voluntary manslaughter. It was an obvious hit and a police officer was killed along with his new bride.

The overzealous D.A. wanted the maximum sentence of 20 years. He claimed Cam chased the man down and killed him after he was no longer a threat. Stein argued for a sentence of ten years with three to serve. It took some doing but in the end the judge sentenced him to five years. Cam was going to prison.

His last few weeks of freedom were spent alone in the darkened condo. The subdued light matched his mood. Besides Trish's mother bringing the kids by Cam was on his own.

The streets were in chaos without him and a united B.C. The power vacuum created mini wars for the lucrative spots Cam abandoned. Ant and Tack fought to maintain their grip on Eastwyck which was still a million dollar trap.

Cam spent his last night on the street talking with Agent Demi. For the first time they did not talk business, this was personal. For the first time they saw each other as people.

The deal Stein worked out called for Cam to turn himself in the day prior to being shipped off to prison. It was meant to spare him the odious conditions of the county jail.

Even the 24 hours he had to spend there were too much. After being dressed in a jail uniform, Cam was taken to the fifth floor. The plan was to get some sleep, but he was put in a cell with a loudmouth. The idiot claimed to know everything and everybody including Cam.

Cam tuned motor mouth out and contemplated his future. His lawyer told him that if he kept his nose clean he could be home in twenty months. It was that hope that prevented him from choking his bunkmate.

He bypassed he slop served for breakfast and boarded the bus to prison. The first stop for all inmates was a diagnostic facility in Midde Georgia.

As soon as the bus stopped at Diagnostics, a team of four huge men in black rushed the bus. They were yelling and cursing putting on a great show of intimidation.

They picked out the largest inmate and demanded he stand. As soon as he did stand they knocked him back down. The four men in black kicked and stomped the defenseless man as he assumed a fetal position.

Cam resolved right then that is anyone of them lay a finger on him, he'd send some wolves to his house. 'Touch me today, die by tonight' he vowed.

The day was a blur of activity as the hundred or so men were herded through the intake process like cattle. They were stripped, shaved, photographed, fingerprinted, weighed, prodded and poked before finally being sent to their living quarters.

The dorm had rows of bunk beds down the sides and middle. Since you weren't allowed to get in them until after 4 P.M., men were strewn about everywhere. As he looked for his assigned bunk his name was called.

"My nigga Cam!" A voice rang out behind him. Cam was relieved to be with someone, anyone that he knew, but when he turned around he strained to recall the almost familiar face.

"It's me! Slim!" his old connect announced with a toothless smile.

Word on the streets had him on the dope and his gums confirmed.

"What's good my nigga!" Cam said genuinely pleased to see him, "What you doing up in here?"

"Shit Shawty, I caught a dime on an a/r," he replied.

"Armed robbery!" Cam laughed. "Nigga who you stuck up?"

"I robbed the dope man. And that nigga called the police!" he exclaimed.

Cam reflected on how quickly and drastically the streets had changed. All day he saw young cats showing off their gunshot wounds. It was as if they were proud of getting holes plugged in, ambulance rides, and extended hospital stays.

Although not much older himself, Cam was a different breed, cut from a different cloth. He didn't take gunshots he gave them. The thought unconsciously sent his hand to his shoulder. He had taken one round but the man who gave it took a few in return. He would not be bragging about shooting Cam.

"I heard you shot up downtown!" Slim laughed showing his tonsils. "They say the mayor and err one was out there."

"Nah, it wasn't that serious," Cam chuckled.

The food in the prison was a hundred times better than the county. Still, Cam had trouble eating it. He gave more of it away than he ate. If it wasn't for the sugar and salt filled commissary items, he would have starved.

Most days were spent taking tests of all sorts. There were a battery of medical and mental evaluations to go through. IQ and spelling tests that Cam breezed through even though most couldn't finish.

Several weeks later the dorm was called back to medical for the results of the AIDS test. Even with 50 men in the small room a pin drop could be heard.

Cam, like everyone was recalling every woman he ever slept with. He cringed at the thought of some of the ones he ran up in raw. Nameless faces, breasts, and vaginas paraded through his mind.

His name had to be repeated twice to break him from the trance. He sat across from the pretty white nurse and stared down at his prison issue boots.

"Well how are you today?" she asked pleasantly.

"You tell me," he chuckled nervously.

"OK, let's see um…

CHAPTER

28

D iagnostic was one drag session after another. Slim kept telling him that once he got into the system it would be better.

Some six months later when his name was called, he was delighted to be moving on. Even though he had a short sentence, the violent crime meant he would at least start his sentence at a close security prison.

He was shipped to North Georgia to Clay State Prison. This one, like the last one had a team of men in black. There were more of them and they were bigger but far less aggressive.

Cam was lucky again to get a bed instead of being sent to the hole. Georgia's prison system was filled to the rafters so bed space was rare. His home would be in D-1, also known as the terror dome.

Since the police tape had just come down, he would be the first one in the room. Two days ago it was a crime scene, today, home.

Cam was exhausted from the long trip and lengthy in process. He only half put his stuff away and stretched out. In his sleep he felt someone in the cell. He sprang from the rack ready to rumble.

"Chill Shawty," Lil D laughed.

"Lil D? My nigga!" Cam exclaimed hugging his homeboy. He hadn't seen the young goon in years. Not since he delivered coke to him at the strip club.

Lil D decided trapping was too much work and tried his hand at armed robbery. His first lick went horribly wrong and ended in murder. He just missed the death penalty and got life without.

After some small talk D took Cam around to meet all the cool people. Still Lil D had a vicious reputation in the system and the introduction meant Cam was untouchable.

"Say Shawty," Cam frowned staring at an older man, "who dat? He look so familiar."

"Oh that's T-Bone," Lil D replied. "He from Decatur too, but he fuck with them boys."

"I know that nigga," Cam swore wracking his brain to place the face.

***

Scoring high on those tests at Diagnostic paid off when it came time to get work assignments. While the dumb niggas were cutting crass and scrubbing pots, Cam was assigned to medical as an orderly.

He almost bucked saying he didn't work for free, but working for free beat a month in the box. Dudes were sitting in the hole praying someone would buck on something, or fight or anything that would free them.

Cam's detail officer was a tiny female guard appropriately names Smalls. Officer Smalls was Cam's age but could pass for 15 with her slight build. He had a hard time believing she was grown, let alone divorced with two kids.

"You 'posed to sweep, mop and wax dese flo's," she ordered when Cam reported. "Take the trash out, don't talk, and you betta not jack on me."

Cam frowned at the jack remark. If there was one single thing that irked him most about prison it was the jackers. Even the sissies stayed in their own lane.

But the jackers! They were everywhere! Everywhere you looks some monkey had his dick out pulling on himself. Cam's first fight came when one refused to put away so he could pass. He was still holding himself when Cam knocked him OUT.

Cam's next thought was why would anybody jack on her? There was nothing to her. No breasts, no ass, nothing.

"Yes ma'am," he said biting his tongue. Their relationship was strictly business but Cam looked for a way in. He knew getting an officer on his team up here would make his stay that much more comfortable.

The doctors and nurses generally went to lunch from 12 to one leaving Cam and Smalls alone. She spent most of her time on the phone arguing with her baby daddy. He was a deadbeat, and Cam knew he could use that to his advantage.

"What's wrong Ms. Smalls," Cam asked when he stumbled across the officer crying at her desk.

"My baby daddy tripping. Again," she sobbed.

Their daily conversation had softened her to the point of being friends.

"What that nigga do?" Cam asked sympathetically.

"These folks gone put me and my babies out if I don't pay them today!" she said fighting back tears.

"How much you owe?" Cam inquired.

"Five hundred dollars!" she exclaimed making it sound like the national debt.

"Here," Cam said scribbling on a piece of paper. "Call this number and tell them I said bring you five hund... no, make it a thousand dollars today."

"Quit playing!" Smalls announced, looking strangely at the paper. "What I gotta do?"

"I ain't playing, and I don't want nothing." Cam said, then moved in for the kill. "I mean we are friends aren't we?"

"Yes." Smalls smiled brightly as she took the number. She meekly relayed Cam's direction. She looked around quickly before passing Cam the phone.

"What's up?" Cam asked.

"So what I'm your do boy?" Demi laughed. "I ain't paying for your tricks."

"Ain't even like that," Cam replied. "Just trying to help. Myself."

**

Officer Smalls was all smiles the next day. After paying her rent she had five hundred extra dollars which probably goes a long way up in the mountains of North Georgia.

She had her hair done in a style from the mid eighties, and a new pair of work boots. When the call for lunch was made Smalls put Cam on the out count and let him stay.

"I ain't posed to do this!" she whispered, handing him a take out container. "So hurry up."

Cam devoured the baby back ribs. He noticed Smalls smiling at him as he ate.

"What?" he inquired between bites.

That's your girlfriend?" she asked with a twinge of jealousy audible in her voice.

"Nah, just friends, why?" he responded.

"Cuz! She talking bout she was jealous of me until she saw me, but she see I ain't your type," Smalls said.

Cam shrugged his shoulders and kept on eating.

"What's wrong with me?" she whined holding up her arms for inspection.

"You're OK, I guess," he said laughing inwardly. He knew the quickest way to the pussy was through the ego.

The following day Smalls sported yet another ancient hair style, but added eyeliner and lip gloss. He knew it what time it was when she told him to stay during lunch.

Cam knew it was time to push the issue, and as soon as the last nurse left, he made his move. He grabbed the officer around her small waist and pulled her close.

As they kissed Cam unbuckled her belt and slid her pants down. He scooped her up and laid her back on the desk. He figured he would have to go easy on the small woman but was surprised when he fell all the way inside her.

The only thing small about Smalls was her name cuz her vagina was huge. Cam chuckled to himself that she was hollow as he stroked her. Big or not it was good. It was the first pussy he'd had in months. He pushed himself all the way in and released his load and tension at the same time.

"Look call Demi, she ha some things for you to bring me," Cam said before pulling out. He knew that with his dick still in her, all she could say was 'OK'.

"OK!" She sang lovingly looking up at Cam. The next day Smalls smuggled in a smart phone complete with chips loaded with the latest music and movies; the day after an ounce of compressed weed and chicken wings.

With the new amenities, time began to fly by. The phone allowed him constant contact with the outside world. He spoke with his kids regularly and through nightly conversations with Demi, they were becoming close.

"Say Shawty,..." Cam began.

"Demi!" she cut in correcting. "How's the GED class?"

"Yeah my bad," he laughed. "Agent, I need you to do some of that agent shit and look dis nigger up."

"Who, and why?" she replied.

150

"They call him T-Bone, but his name tag say Tyrone Butler. As for the why, I don't know. I dream about this dude. I'm somehow connected to Shawty," Cam explained.

"Dreamed!" Demi exclaimed. "You been in there too long!"

"You tripping," Cam laughed. "No homo Shawty, matter fact you need to stop fronting and send me a picture of that coochie."

"Boy stop," she laughed. "I already told you about that. I'll let you see her right before you kiss her."

"Count time, I gotta go," Cam laughed as he disconnected the phone.

CHAPTER
29

"Got that info you requested. Tyrone Butler, a/k/a Fly Tye, a/k/a Tye Tye; age 50 serving twelve years on voluntary manslaughter," Demi said reading from the file.

"OK, I still can't figure out where I know dis nigga from," Cam said frustrated. "So who the nigga kill?"

"He choked some girl he was dating. He was a suspect in a couple more similar attacks but the D.A. couldn't prove them," she replied.

Cam was in shock. He disconnected the call and sat on his rack deep in thought. Tears streamed down his face as the painful memories replayed in his head.

"Fuck wrong with you?" Lil D asked as he came in and saw his hero distressed.

"I found the nigga that killed my momma," Cam whispered.

"Who?" 'D' whispered back.

"Downstairs, that nigga T-Bone. That's Tye, he killed my momma," Cam said shaking his head.

"Let's go murk that nigga!" Lil D announced. He pulled a huge shank from it's hiding place and went for the door.

"Not yet," Cam said physically restraining the man.

I wanna hear him say it," Cam fumed. "I want the nigga to admit it."

One thing Cam noticed about niggas in jail is that they love to talk. Love to brag about shit they did and lie about shit they haven't done. Niggas talk so much that other niggas get indicted from them running their mouths.

Cam spent the next few days under Tye. He made up all kinds of wild tales of crimes and bodies. He had plenty of real stories under his belt, but all of the things Cam was, stupid was not one of them.

Tye fell right into it and ran his mouth for days. According to him, he was the biggest dealer the city of Atlanta had ever seen. The most ruthless killer with bodies scattered from Douglasville to Stone Mountain.

"You ain't never kilt no hoe," Cam dared knowing that if he did he'd tell it.

"The hell I ain't," Tye said chomping on the bait. "Shit! Plenty!"

Cam twisted his lips in a 'yeah right' fashion urging the man to go on.

"That's what I'm down fo now! Choked a bitch out!" he exclaimed. "'Tween me and you I did one back in the day. Little young fuck I had. Suck a dick like nobody's business.

Cam fought to contain the rage that slowly built inside of him. He felt his blood literally begin to boil as Tye spoke.

"Yeah Shawty done clipped me for my whole bomb! You know I had to see bout t he bitch," Tye bragged.

"So what you did?" Cam asked bracing himself for the reply. He half hoped it wouldn't be his mother but when Tye spoke it was exactly how he remembered it.

"I fed a couple sacks to her girl to set her up. I got up in there and bitch all sorry and I'll suck ya dick. So I let her. As soon as I nutted in that hoe mouth I choked her stank ass out with my belt. I look up and the lil bitch son sitting there staring at me. I started to kill his ass too!" Tye laughed.

"You should have," Cam said ominously before getting up and walking off.

The very next morning Cam and Lil D slipped inside of Tye's cell just after first count. Tye's bunkmate worked in the kitchen so they had him to themselves.

Lil D wanted to make the most of the four hours til next count, and torture him. Since the dorm was quiet at that hour torture would make too much noise.

Besides, Cam wasn't up for the theatrics. Murder was about killing, plain and simple.

Cam slipped his belt around Tye's neck as he slept. Lil D woke him up with a poke from the shank. To prevent him from screaming, he pulled the belt tight.

"Shhh!" Cam whispered in his ear. "Uh uh, don't bitch up now."

"What... what y'all niggas want?" Tye pleaded. He couldn't understand why death was waking him up this morning. "I got a couple sticks in my box."

"Nigga don't nobody want yo weed Shawty," Lil D growled, sticking him again.

Again Cam tightened the belt to muffle his cries.

"You know that 'lil bitch' you choked? Huh? Cam demanded choking and releasing as he spoke. "In front of her son? The one you shoulda killed?"

"What that got to do with you Shawty?" Tye pleaded desperately.

"That lil boy was me! That 'lil bitch' was my momma!" Cam spat as he squeezed. "Shoulda killed me too."

This time Cam didn't let up. Tye kicked and clawed as the life slipped away from him. When his eyes took on that 'faraway' look of death, Cam released his hold.

"Go on Shawty, I got it from here," Lil D said urgently.

Cam wasn't sure what he meant, but removed the belt from the dead man's neck and slipped out of the room. He used a new razor blade to shred the belt and flush it down the toilet.

A loud commotion brought Cam along with the rest of the dorm out of the cells. It was Lil D dragging Tye's now bloody corpse out of the cell.

"Y'all niggas see dis shit!" he demanded holding the shank high. "Dis what you get for running your mouth!"

The stunned guard in the control room frantically called the code as 'Lil D' repeatedly stabbed the dead man.

155

"I did this! Anybody else want it?" He yelled daring one of Tye's lovers or friends to come help.

Lil D was rushed by the men in black and cuffed up. He was still taking responsibility for the murder as they drug him off.

"Fuck the free world! Chain gang for life!" were his final words.

With Tye being stabbed so many times, in front of guards, Cam was completely distanced from the crime.

With all the bodies under Cam's belt, for some reason this one shook him up. He sat on his bunk and wept uncontrollably. He killed before but it was business, this was personal and it affected him. Lil D was already never getting out as another life sentence wouldn't hurt none. Cam had a life. He had another chance at life and knew he had to get himself together. He had millions offshore thanks to Stein. It was now time to work on his soul.

Cam went to the church call out that evening looking for salvation. He sat in the back, where he thought he belonged. He thought wrong as the men around him began giving each other hand jobs.

What he didn't know is that the sissy's used church service to hook up. They figured they were going to hell anyway so why not? Disgusted, Cam went back to the dorm.

When he got into his cell a young dude was already in there unpacking his belongings. He looked up when Cam walked in.

"Sup you?" The youngin said extending his hand.

"What you call me? Cam asked as he gave him a pound.

"You, I said what's up you," he repeated.

"Cam Shawty, call me Cam," Cam explained.

That's what's up you. Call me 'You'," You replied without a hint of sarcasm.

His name was Yunus but everyone called him You, and he in return called everyone you.

"So what you one of dem Muslims," Cam inquired at the obvious since a prayer rug hung from the bed and a crisp white kufi adorned his head.

"Yeah, but I'm a real Muslim!" He announced adamantly. "I ain't one of dese can I have a soup ass Muslims running round here!"

"A what?" Cam chuckled.

"Can I have a soup, you know they be like As-alaamu Alaykum can I have a soup. Niggas be fronting!"

Cam just laughed. He had noticed that all the chain gang religions were full of hypocrites. The church dudes had some sissy's sneaking around, the Muslims had cowards just seeking protection. Everything was a hustle.

You and Cam became fast friends. Muslim or not, 'You' liked he same weed and music as Cam. He wouldn't take any of the baby back ribs Smalls bought in but was down for everything else.

He was from the west side of Atlanta where his father was the Imam. His father and some brothers from the Masjid

157

made it their business to run all criminals from their neighborhood.

Except You. He was a goon just like the rest of his hood. He as only 18 but a vet already. He beat an armed robbery and murder charge but not the gun charge. If all went well, he'd be home the same time as Cam.

You alluded to some sweet big money licks, minus details since Cam insisted he wasn't down. Cam took the youngster under his wing and planned to give him a job in whatever lay ahead for himself. It would be legal though cuz Cam and officially sworn off the thug life.

CHAPTER

30

"Where's Officer Small's?" Cam asked when he reported to detail.

"She pregnant so they put her in the annex," his new detail officer replied. She was a cute black girl, but big. She was also know to be police. Cam just knew his extras had come to an end. She wasn't bringing shit.

Officer Lawrence was a true fat girl. She wasn't one of those 'I'm a little heavy', or 'trying to lose a few', she was a proud fat girl. Fly too – in all the latest fashions that she could find in her size.

Food dominated her conversation. All she spoke of was tender meats falling off the bone, or cream fillings, or glazes of some sort. Fat girl for real.

Work was just work without all the extras and time began to drag. He and Demi had grown to the point of planning a future. They spoke nightly so she would be the one to break the news.

"Well baby," Demi sighed before continuing, "I have good news and bad news."

"Bad first," Cam frowned, hoping the good would compensate for the bad.

"Well… Stein passed," she said solemnly.

"Fuck!" Cam exclaimed. "Shawty got all my bread."

"Well, worry about that when you get home. You made parole," Demi stated.

It took him a while to process what he just heard. After twenty-two long months, Cam was coming home.

After being processed out they handed him a check for $35.00. He stared at the paltry sum and wondered what in the world anyone could do with $35.00. Even if you spent the last twenty years down, all the state had for you was $35.00.

"I ain't I 'posed to get a bus ticket?" Cam inquired as they led him to the gate.

"You got a ride," the guard said plainly.

Cam did a double take to make sure his eyes weren't lying. Agent Demi was always professionally dressed. Business suits or slacks at all times.

But there stood Demi in a miniskirt, halter top and 'fuck me pumps'. She was leaning against a new Charger with a wicked grin.

"Not you looking like a hoochie mama!" Cam laughed as he approached.

"Trying to make you feel at home," she laughed.

The couple shared their first kiss right there in the prison parking lot. They made love for the first time in the nearest motel. After a romantic evening they made the two hour drive to Atlanta.

"So this is where you stay. Nice!" Cam complimented when he entered Demi's condo for the first time.

"I'm glad you like it, especially since you helped pay for it," she smiled.

She gave him the tour, stopping to show him the new wardrobe she purchased for him.

"Oh yeah, the Charger's yours too," she said tossing him the keys.

"Preciate it," Cam said solemnly.

"I can't tell!" Demi frowned. "I just broke you off with a new car with all the bells and whistles and you got your head down.

"Worried about my bread Shawty," he admitted. "With Stein dead I don't even know where to begin.."

"Well it won't be too hard to find. First things first – go see your kids," Demi urged.

Trisha's mother had moved into the house with the kids when Cam went away. Since it was in the kids' names anyway he told her to stay. He couldn't believe how much they grew in his absence. Even the baby was running around talking.

Cam's next step was Decatur to see his kids by Shay and Britney. Britney had since had another and was working on a third. He took them all out shopping and left.

After catching up with his kids he went down to Stein's office. He sat there for an hour staring at the 'for lease' sign in the window. All he had for his two $2.4 mil were a couple of numbered account books from parts unknown.

He still owned the building that once housed his club but it was tied up in ongoing litigation. A couple of patrons got hit by strays and sued.

Cam planned to go legit. He tried but he needed money. "A quick mil and I'ma chill" he told his reflection.

He pulled out his phone and dialed a new number.

"As-Salaamu Alaykum, who dis?" You barked.

"Sup You," Cam laughed. "This Cam."

"Chillin you, you ready to get this money?" he asked.

"I'm listening," he shot back.

"Swing through, You said and hung up.

***

The west side of Atlanta is the hood. Trappers and jackers as far as the eye can see. Typical depressing ghetto landscape until you turned to Hill St. This is where the Muslims lived. They had a ten block area in each direction. The houses were clean and freshly painted and maintained. The grass was cut and the hedges were trimmed. Clean children played safely in the streets.

Cam pulled the Charger to a stop at the address given and turned off the ignition. Before he stepped out the car he was met by a large man with a big beard and what had to an A/R 15 or AK under his white robe.

"Can I help you?" He asked menacingly and pleasant at the same time.

"Looking for my nigga You," Cam said knowing the word nigga wouldn't be appreciated.

"Say my nigga!" You said loudly stepping towards him. "Chill Mustapha, this my people!"

Yunus took Cam downstairs to his basement apartment. He locked the door behind them and lit a blunt of exotic herbs that sweetened the air.

"So what's the biz Shawty," Cam asked between tokes.

"As you can see, my daddy and dem run this whole section," You began exhaling a plume of weed smoke. "Them Jamaican blood clot ass niggas moved in 'round the corner selling weed, and blow."

"So! Niggas can't sell no weed or blow around here?" Cam asked naively.

"No! Not around here! Not where my lil sister and dem play. My momma walking around!" You said hotly. "Fuck no!"

"I feel you Shawty," Cam replied sincerely. He did feel him in fact. He often wondered why black folk ate where they shit.

Wondered why they turned their own hoods into ghettos. White people didn't do that. Neither did the Chinese or Vietnamese, and obviously not the Muslims either.

"I'm saying though Shawty, how that gone help me," Cam asked plainly.

"My daddy and dem finna run up in there and murk dem niggas," You stated. "We done asked them nicely and they won't go."

"So, um, how that help me?" Cam repeated.

"They gonna go up in there and kill dem and leave all the dope and money. That's how they do it. They leave all dat for the police, they want that ass!" You explained.

"I still don't get it," Cam exclaimed.

"Nigga we gone lay on the move! As soon as they hit, we run in, grab the work and bread! I know for a fact they got keys up in there."

"Tell me when," Cam announced, "I'm in!"

✱✱✱

The next night Cam squatted in the woods staking out the Jamaicans' house. You overheard the plans and was in perfect position.

"Here we go," he whispered as a Muslim slipped into the backyard. He aimed an SKS at the back door and keyed his walkie talkie. That was the signal and all hell broke loose.

You's father and two other brothers kicked the front door. The Jamaicans were vets and always on the alert. Atlanta is the home invasion capitol of the south and they were ready.

Ready, but outgunned. A shotgun blast from the lead Muslim lifted a dread off his feet and landed him in the next room. The other man raised a chopper but was almost cut in half as the Imam let loose with his A/R 15.

The only Jamaican with a brain hit the back door. He leaped the back steps but the brother caught him in midair. When he landed half his brain was still on the porch.

Cam's dick was hard! He loved his gangsta shit. You literally had to hold him back until it was time to move.

"Now!" You ordered as soon as the brother left the yard.

They hopped over the brain matter on the back porch and stormed into the room. They still had the guns raised on the lookout for survivors or hiders.

There was a kilo on the counter being prepared to be cooked. Cam swept it into his bag and followed You into the house.

"Jackpot!" He announced as they entered a room holding more dope.

"We gonna need a bigger bag," Cam laughed as he stuffed brick after 2.2 pound brick into the satchel.

You found a bag filled with bundles of cash and threw it over his shoulder. They prepared to leave but hit one last room on the way out.

"Fuck!" Cam exclaimed at the sight.

The Jamaicans weren't just dope dealers they were gunrunners. The room had an arsenal of weapons they couldn't identify.

Already heavily laden hey grabbed boxes of grenades and a crate of machine guns. If they had more time they would have cleaned the room out but after the barrage of gunfire police would be arriving soon.

Cam had to physically restrain You from going back in for more guns. What neither man new was how much and how soon they would need the extra fire power,

CHAPTER
31

The lick netted the two men fifty kilos of blow, seventy five thousand in cash, thirty anti-personal grenades and a crate of twenty submachine guns. Cam knew if he put all that work on the street it would net millions.

He decided to take his young partner in crime out to celebrate and he knew just the place.

When Cam and You arrived at Demi's condo she was rushing out. The bulletproof vest and shoulder holster took You by surprise.

"You okay?" Cam asked troubled by the troubled look on her face.

"No, all hell broke loose downtown. I won't be back tonight," Demi said trading a peck on the lips before rushing off.

"What your old lady police!" You exclaimed.

"Nah she ain't no police!" Cam replied indignantly. "She DEA!"

***

When they pulled up to Charles' club there were all new faces. New doormen who didn't know Cam and had to walkie talkie approval.

New bartenders who didn't know to set out a bottle of champagne on sight. And best of all new dancers to take to V.I.P. and gut!

"My nigga!" Charles said embracing Cam in a bear hug. "When you touch the turf?"

"Just now Shawty," Cam replied. "Gone be back on in a sec."

"Yeah I know how you do it!" Charles said eagerly. He ordered the private V.I.P. cleared and sent champagne and four girls he knew the men would like.

Cam and You lit separate blunts and reclined as the girls arrived. In walked four of the prettiest, well built women in the world.

Two were short, dark, and pretty. The other two light skinned Amazons. Instead of dancing the girls began eating each other. The formed two 60 sessions as the men smoked.

"Fuck this!" You exclaimed before stripping and joining them on the floor.

The poor fellow couldn't decide what to do, so he alternated between them all. Cam declined the offer to join and was deep in thought.

A lot had changed in the couple of years he was gone. Add to that all the time he spent off the streets making moves behind the scene.

Now he had to get back in the trenches. He had to reestablish his rep and take back what was once his; and he knew no one would just lay down for him.

Since no one would lay down for Cam, You had a crew of wolves that laid niggas down. Tonight was party and bullshit, tomorrow world war three.

Demi was pacing the floor like a caged tiger when Cam returned. As soon as he walked in she confronted him.

"Tell me you're not involved!" she demanded, poking his chest with a finger.

"OK, I'm not involved," he replied with a shrug. "I was a the club all night."

"So why is your car at a fucking murder scene," she demanded. She handed him surveillance photos of his Charger charging away.

"This on the west side!" He replied dumbfounded.

"I know good and damn well where it is! I set up the damn camera!" she screamed.

"Shit Shawty I was down there chillin' with You and …

"With me?" Demi asked puzzled.

"No not you! My nigga You! That's his name… anyway so me and You chillin' when we hear shots. That's why you see me peeling. Trying not to get shot!" He said worthy of an award.

"This is crazy!" Demi said collapsing on the sofa. "We had been watching them for weeks. We know them Muslims were involved, but they never take drugs and money. Never!"

"First time for everything," Cam shrugged.

"We don't care about the money, or dope. They got our guns!" Demi sighed.

✳✳✳

"Cam? My nigga! What's poppin Shawty," Ant said cheerfully upon taking his old boss' call.

"I'm home," Cam sang, "ready to pick up where we left off.

Cam frowned at the awkward silence. His old friend should be more than happy to get back to work.

"We straight Shawty," Ant finally replied dismissively.

"Straight?" He repeated. "What you mean straight?"

"I'm saying I took over after you left, so you know, I'm straight. But if you need some money I can hit you with a lil pack, just get me my dough. You know how we do it."

Cam couldn't believe his ears. Here was his home boy fronting on him in the trap that he established. He felt his blood beginning to boil as the conversation went on.

"OK, so I tell you what," Cam began calmly, "since the trap still bumping I'm send a team over there to work."

"Over where? Here?" Ant asked dripping with hostility. "Nah Shawty, I wouldn't do dat. You do I'm send them right back."

"OK! That's what's up," Cam laughed. "Hey, I'll check you later."

He disconnected and turned to You. You gave him an 'I told you so look' as he stood. In fact he had told him so. He wondered what made his mentor think niggas were just gonna lay down cuz he came back. It was all good though cuz You wanted to lay them down his self, and now he had the green light.

✳✳✳

"Man I told dat fuck nigga if I catch him round here I'm slap fire from his ass!" Ant bragged to his workers.

"What he say?" One of the eager young boys asked. Cam was a legend in Eastwyck, To be in the company of the man who "took" his trap and chumped him off.

"That nigga ain't say shit!" Ant laughed. "That nigga ain't crazy!"

As they spoke two of the front windows broke simultaneously. The five men inside looked oddly at the strange metal balls that came in the holes. One man bent to look at it when it exploded.

The second grenade exploded just after the first, annihilating those closest to them. Ant and another survivor stumbled wounded out the front door.

You smiled as the submachine ripped the two men to shreds. The war had begun. Eastwyck was only the first battle. Cam had a couple million to make and vowed no one could eat until he made them.

Dealers all over the east side were given three options. You could either work Cam's package, take a vacation or die.

Even You was surprised how many chose to die. Him and his crew took Decatur over one apartment complex at a time. From Candler, to Glenwood, to Memorial Drive, it was war.

Meanwhile Cam cooked coke. He employed the whip game he mastered, and cooked batch after batch of crack. He had a mountain of crack by the end of the day.

***

"Baby this thing is out of control!" Demi confided. "They shot it out with the local police today. Those bastards threw a grenade.!"

"Shawty you need to quit," Cam said kissing her forehead. I got a few things working. I'ma have all my bread back then we leaving Atlanta."

"Mmm," she moaned enjoying the affection. "You right too. I definitely need to quit if I'm pregnant."

"What make you say that?" he asked sitting up suddenly."

"Period late," Demi said calmly. "I ain't never been late."

You's people moved into every trap they took over. It still took a small army to protect the workers. Even when police rolled up, they were met with a hail of gunfire.

"Y'all niggas gone stand for this?" Nard growled. He called a meeting of dudes who ordinarily would be rivals, but now shared a common fore. They came to an agreement to fight fire with fire. They spoke the only language the hood knows, violence.

As the war raged on, local police stepped back. They had lost too many men already. Shooting unarmed black men was their specialty. It was no fun when they shot back.

Finally the DEA was forced to take over. These superior surveillances led them to a house on Line Street. Plans were drawn up and they intended to end the war once and for all.

CHAPTER

32

D emi just shook her head at the test strip. This one had a happy face. The one before that showed two lines and the one before that a plus sign. No doubt about it, she was pregnant.

Cam sat in the next room contemplating his fate. He was tripping and he knew it. He tried to put the boo down on a whole city. As a result he was engaged in an all out war.

No one was winning. No one could sell no dope cuz they were too busy busting their guns. They had managed to grind out a mil in between fire fights. He planned to make an offer he couldn't refuse.

He looked at the shiny diamond engagement ring and smiled. He thought about rushing in there and dropping to one knee and asking Demi now. In the end he decided to stick with the plan.

They had reservations for tomorrow night. That's when he would tell her he was out. Out for good and ask her to become his wife.

Demi played in the bathroom mirror seeing what she would look like in a few months. She stuck her hard stomach out and laughed. She knew her man had a lot on his mind so she decided to wait before telling him. He made dinner reservations for the next day so that would be the perfect time.

Cam cringed as he neared the Line Street house. One of the reasons he'd been so successful in the game is because he was smart. He very rarely put himself around drugs. Now here he was going to a house full of drugs, money and guns.

Common sense overwhelmed him causing him to circle the block. He parked on the next street and cut through the backyards to the house.

"Got a deal for you," Cam told his young protégé.

"Talk to me," You said eagerly.

"We got one point two in cash right now plus twice that worth in work." He said pausing to let You absorb the statement.

"Let me walk with a mil, the rest is yours," he offered.

"Don't tell me all dis gangsta shit getting to you!" You laughed.

"Matter fact it is," Cam confided to his own surprise. "Ain't feeling it no more."

"That's what's up," You nodded, "but don't try to come back when you see a nigga ballin!"

The two friends shared a laugh and a hug. When they separated Cam began loading his mil in a large tote bag. He

175

was up to three hundred thousand when the first stun grenade came through the window.

You had thrown enough grenades in the last month to know what to do. He dove for Cam knocking them both down. Once the flash bang device exploded You threw a real grenade.

"Come on you," You said leading Cam out a side window.

They landed right in front of the two agents assigned to prevent escape from the side as a vicious fire fight raged on behind them.

Cam and You both raised their weapons at the agents who did the same. Cam and Demi locked eyes with their guns drawn and froze. That hesitation was enough for Demi's partner to shoot.

You dove in front of Cam squeezing off automatic gunshots. He grunted as the agents' slugs tore through his chest. The male agent's forehead opened up as You's rounds reached it.

"I got 'em," he said spitting up blood from his tattered lungs.

Cam pushed him off and scrambled to Demi. Her eyes were wide open but she couldn't see him. Dead people can't see anything.

Radio chatter came closer signaling Cam that he had to leave. He crawled using his hands and feet til it was safe to stand. He sprinted full speed taking the back fence like a track hurdle.

He made it to his car and pulled off fighting the urge to floor it. Two blocks over he began passing police cars rushing to join the fight. He tossed his pistol out before turning onto Glenwood.

Knowing the DEA would soon be swarming over their fallen agent's residence, Cam quickly loaded what he could grab. He had a couple thousand in cash plus the worthless account books from Stein, and a pistol.

Cam jumped on 20 west and rode until he could no longer keep his eyes open. He pulled into a motel and grabbed a room. He collapsed on the bed and passed out. In the morning he was the top story.

CHAPTER

33

"Georgia authorities are calling last night's shootout the deadliest in history. Armed drug dealers engaged in an hour long gun battle with federal agents.

A drug raid turned deadly as the occupants of a Decatur, GA stash house opened fire on agents. Five agents are among the dead along with eight suspects.

Neighbors say it sounded like a war complete with bombs and explosions."

"That shit is mad gangsta!" Easy announced loudly, as the news report showed the stash house.

It truly looked as if a war had been waged there. All the windows were gone along with the doors. Half the roof was burned off from the ensuing fire. The Red brick façade was riddled with pot marks from tens of thousands of rounds fired at it.

Chris sat up and watched as faces of the dead agents graced the screen. The faces of the bad guys were shown next with the caption 'deceased' across their mug shots.

"One suspect authorities believe fled the scene is still at large. "Cameron Forrest is said to be armed and extremely dangerous. The convicted killer ...""

"Would you look a this bitch ass nigga!" Chris said hotly.

"Is that who I think it is?" Easy asked. "That nigga I we was beefing with?"

"Yeah that's him," Chris snarled, "the nigga that killed Bo-Bo."

"Got Ervin and Lisa too," Easy reminded him of the failed hit.

"Should have did that shit myself," Chris said shaking his head.

He had the drop on Cam the night at the club but didn't act. He chided himself about using the hit team instead of handling his own business. No, he had to be all dramatic, sending champagne and shit.

"That's the nigga that knocked Bo off? And your hit team," Trey asked incredulously. "Same nigga gave you that limp?"

***

A pain shot through Chris' leg at the mention of his limp. It was indeed courtesy of Cam on the yacht. Just as Chris leaped from the boat, two rounds impacted his leg. One passed through harmlessly. The other gave him a limp for life.

"That nigga! How y'all let some young ass nigga wet y'all," Trey chuckled.

Trey had two severely bad problems, both were his mouth. He did not know when to shut up. He proved his worth as a gunman but his mouth was about to get him into trouble.

"Ayo, chill son!" Easy warned. He saw his cousin's face change and knew Chris well enough to know what that meant.

"Chill what!!! How y'all let some clown ass nigga kill y'all?" Precious, Bo-Bo, Er...

Boom!!

"You!" Chris said standing over Trey's corpse, "you forgot about you, big mouth ass nigga."

Easy just laughed. He knew Trey's bit mouth was gonna get him killed one day. Silly nigga was so busy insulting him he didn't see Chris approach him with a gun. He was in mid-sentence when Chris put two in his head. He'd have to finish telling that story in hell.

"So how you wanna play this?" Easy asked warily. He knew his friend was a maniac. Chris had no brakes. There was nothing he wouldn't do.

His mind flashed back to the early 90s when Chris went after a worker that stole from the family. It wasn't the two grand that got the man in trouble. They spent that much at the bar on a Monday night.

The fact that anyone had the balls to steal from them is what cost him. It was the principle. Dude knew he fucked up and offered to work it off. Chris agreed but he heard the tone and took flight.

Chris killed his brother, sister, two cousins, and dog before Dude got the message. He drove back from his North Carolina hideout to let Chris kill him. He knew his mother an grandparents were next.

"You know how I get down B," Chris said ominously. "You know son hiding. We gotta flush him out! Until then it's business as usual."

CHAPTER

34

B usiness as usual was selling cocaine and lots of it. When Chris emerged on the Miami shore with bullets in his leg he was officially in charge.

He'd seen Bo get splattered before he bolted. He planned to take revenge, but first had to get the word out that he was the man.

Chris drove all the way back from South Florida before seeing a doctor. He arrived at Bo's Long Island mansion and kicked the door open.

"What's wrong?" Bo's girl Maria screamed at the intrusion. Of all the women they ran through, they all had a man girl. A bottom bitch and Maria was Bo's.

The former Ms. Dominican Republic was drop dead gorgeous and built like a brick shit house.

"Bo dead! Chris announced roughly.

"Noooo!" Maria screamed covering her face with her hands.

She rushed into his arms looking for some compassion. She found none.

Instead of embracing the grieving woman Chris tuned her around and bent her over. He lifted her nightgown over her head and forced himself inside of her.

"I run the show now!" He growled. "Everything now belongs to me! The business! The house! The cars are mine!

"Mmm this pussy yours too!! Maria moaned. "You the man!"

After fucking Bo-Bo's woman, Chris showered in his bathroom and dressed in his clothes. As Maria cooked for him Chris ordered all of the crew's lieutenants and their second in command to an emergency meeting.

"All the LT's put up your hands!" Chris demanded.

Reluctantly they did what they were told to do. None of them particularly liked or respected the man but they feared him.

Chris removed a nine millimeter pistol and shot each one of them in the head.

"Bo is dead!" He announced to the shocked survivors. "Who is in charge!"

"You are!" The remaining men sounded off in unison.

The new organization was a force to be reckoned with. They established themselves in every borough of New York City. Still Chris had more ambitious plans. He wanted to expand. It wasn't business, this was personal. He put together a team and headed south. Destination Atlanta.

CHAPTER

35

C am awoke the morning after the shootout in a dingy motel room. He could only shake his head as channel after channel ran footage and reports of the gun battle that took everything away from him.

When he returned to the condo to grab whatever he could, he saw the positive pregnancy test. Not only did he lose his girl, but his unborn child as well. Killed by his own protégé who tried to save him.

He knew the slugs that dropped 'You' were meant for him. The scene replayed in his mind on an endless loop. If he could go back he'd gladly have died with Demi.

Faces of the men and women he sent to an early death began to flash through his mind. A parade of the murdered led by Black, Scoop, Aunt Ebony, followed by Octavius and the no names driver, Shay, Weasel and Tye.

He thought about all the bodies that fell on his command. All the casualties of the turf ware he started. Death overwhelmed him as he raised his pistol to his temple. His finger tightened around the trigger slowly raising the hammer.

Another thought flashed in his mind putting the self murder on hold. A far stronger emotion filled the convoluted mind. The thought of vengeance rushed into his whole being.

From that second on his life was about the get back. Chris and anyone near him had to die. Revenge was the only thing that now mattered.

"From six mil to thirty grand!" He laughed upon counting his cash. He placed the gun back into the bag on top of the money and the useless bank books. He still had no idea what language was written on them.

"Scuse me sir," Cam said politely attempting to tear the elderly motel clerk away from his soaps. "Is there a library over here?"

"Ova on Maple," he replied only glancing up for a second at his guest. He then did a double take to study Cam's face.

"Maple sir?" Cam smiled while inwardly frowning. The double take unnerved him.

"Turn left outa here, right on Maple, can't miss it," he explained. The curious clerk watched Cam as he got into his car and took note of the George tag as he pulled out. He then turned back to his stories wondering where he'd seen the man before.

***

Cam wished he would have taken Demi up on her frequent attempts to teach him how to navigate on the internet. He was street savvy but knew nothing about modern technology. He did however, know that the internet would be the best place to start his search. He knew he needed help in his plans for revenge and knew just who to recruit.

A young girl seated at one of the small library's three computers eyed Cam flirtatiously as he walked. She knew he wasn't from the area and even in his disheveled state he put all the locals to shame.

Cam noticed the pretty girl but dismissed her in the same instant. He had bigger fish to fry and plus she was too young. He sat down at the terminal and tried his best to figure it out.

He looked over at the girl's screen where she was surfing, chatting, and social networking at the same time. She was maneuvering so quickly Cam figured she had to know what she was doing.

After a few minutes of getting nowhere, he accepted defeat and asked for help.

"Say Shawty," Cam leaned in and whispered, "how you goggle a nigga?"

"Goggle? You mean Google," she laughed getting prettier as she did. The girlish giggle revealed she was a lot younger than her well developed body indicated.

"Yeah Google," Cam laughed looking at the old photograph in his hand. The name and the face on the picture was Cam's but it was taken the year before he was born.

"He got a Facebook?" She asked pulling up the media giant on the screen.

"A what?" Cam asked ignorantly.

"Facebook?... Really? Never mind, what's his name?" she asked.

"Cameron," he replied, "Cameron Forrest.

"Wow! Lots of them! She said as he results popped onto the screen.

She scrolled through the unfamiliar faces until one came into view that was familiar. He double checked the image on the screen against the picture in his palm.

"That's him!" Cam said feeling a rush of emotions as the picture of the father he'd never met smiled back at him.

"New York!" the girl exclaimed. "Give me your name and I'll send him a message."

"Tell him Cameron," he replied, "his son."

"OK, what's your number?" she sang as she in-boxed the message.

"Shit, I ain't got no phone!" Cam said remembering he wisely tossed his out before leaving Atlanta. "How long it take to get the message?"

"Just depends on how often he be on here," she said before pulling up his history. "Um looks like err day. He was just on a few minutes ago."

"Give him your number," Cam instructed causing the young girl to look up at him.

"OK but you gotta buy me something to eat," she negotiated.

"Deal! What's your name Shawty," Cam asked as they stood to leave.

"Tywanna," she smiled flirtatiously. "What's yours?"

"Ca… um… just call me Mike," he replied. He was flattered by the young girl's flirting but even in the best of circumstances she was too young. 'Sixteen tops' he mused to himself even though she had the build of a woman.

"Here yo lil ass is!" A much older man yelled as soon as they emerged from the library. "Brang your ass here!"

Cameron assumed he was her father by his tone and age. He knew he couldn't intervene in a family matter, but still needed to get that call.

"Un uh Willie! I ain't going nowhere with you!" Tywanna shrieked hiding behind Cam.

"Look man, I don't wanna get in yo business! Cam began meekly.

"So don't," the man said approaching. "I bought this lil bitch and she run off fo I even get her home."

"Bought?" Cam said in disbelief. "Look all I ne…

The man's open handed slap prevented him from finishing the sentence. Cam knew he was wanted and the absolute last thing he needed was to get caught in the middle of a domestic dispute.

The fact that this forty something man had 'bought' a child had him hot, but the slap was unforgivable.

People were beginning to look over at the scene which was quickly getting out of hand. A sweet piece dropped the man to one knee, and a well placed kick put him to sleep.

"Can't believe I'ma get fucked up over some bullshit!" Cam fumed as he sped off, "fuck was that about?"

"My momma a junkie! She tried to sell me to that man," Tywanna said beginning to cry.

Cam felt for her but had to leave. He decided to ditch the girl first chance he got.

"Say Shawty, walk back up to that burger joint and get us something to eat," he demanded handing her a crisp hundred dollar bill.

"Walk!" She exclaimed. "That's too far."

"Leave the phone in case my people come, I'ma jump in the shower," he demanded, walking in the bathroom before she could reply.

Cam tried to shower quickly so he could leave before she returned. He lathered up and was finishing off when he heard the room's door creak open. "Fuck it," he said intending to dismiss her once and for all.

When he walked out the bathroom he elderly clerk was holding a double barreled shotgun.

"I knew I sent you," he chuckled pleased with himself, "you been on the news! They got money on yo head boy!"

"I got money too," Cam said raising his hands. "In that bag right there. Let me go and you can have it."

"Gone take it and get the reward," the greedy clerk laughed.

"Just check it out! Dump it out on the bed," Cam urged. He planned to make a play for his gun as soon as it hit he bed.

"OK, but you move I swear 'fo God I'ma open a hole in ya big nuff to drive a tractor through.

The man's eyes grew large as the bundles of cash tumbled out onto the bed. Cam's eyes did too when no gun came out.

"Shut my mouth!" the clerk exclaimed. It was only thirty grand but more money than he'd seen at one time in his whole life.

As Cam puzzled at where his gun went, the front door eased open and in came his answer.

"Put it down mister!" Tywanna demanded holding the large weapon in her small hand.

Cam began to ease up as the clerk turned his attention to the girl.

"Gal put that gun down!" he demanded. His tone was so commanding she began to lower the gun as instructed.

Knowing he had to get the gun before him Cam sprang into action. The clerk saw the move and raised the canon to shoot.

At the same time Tywanna lifted her gun, closed her eyes and squeezed the trigger.

The round caught the man in his temple and took a chunk of his forehead off as it exited. Cam wasted no time. He scooped his money back into the bag and rushed out of the room.

He slid into his car wearing only a towel and started the engine. Before he could pull off Tywanna was right behind him.

"Give me the gun!" Cam demanded of the girl who was oddly calm.

"I dropped it," she replied. "That man dead?"

Cam looked at her strangely at the question. She had to see the man's scalp on the ceiling as they left.

"How old are you?" Cam finally asked.

"Well... I'ma be seventeen ... birthday after this next one," she said painting a mathematical equation out of the question."

"15! Your 15?" Cam exclaimed.

"Technically yes, 15," she replied nodding. "We going to New York?"

"Yeah," Cam replied, heading the last place anyone would expect him. The last place he expected to be.

CHAPTER

36

"**O**h God Demi!" Agent Wilson exclaimed as he walked into his deceased partner's condo.

Anthony Wilson was a rising star in the agency, on the fast track to management. When he was paired with Demi he could hardly contain himself. He had a huge crush on her since they went through the academy. Now as his knees buckled upon entering her condo he realized just how much he loved her.

He had even been covering her with the supervisors who couldn't understand why she could never get anything on the elusive Cameron Forrest.

Wilson himself headed the New York leg of the joint operation. His association with Bo-Bo and Chris meant Cam was certainly a drug dealer. He proved that much on the side.

Two steps into the condo Wilson frowned at its lavish accoutrements. The unit itself was in the three hundred thousand range but the living room held a ten thousand dollar leather sectional.

The huge salt water fish tank setup ran another ten, and the carpet was so plush it threatened to swallow his loafers.

Marble, crystal, and imported stone decked out the fireplace. A slight smile began to spread as the agent neared the pictures on the mantle.

A smiling Demi stood front and center, but next to it was Demi and a man. The way they held each other said they were deeply in love. The agent could not believe who the man turned out to be.

"Forrest?" He questioned, questioning his own eyes. The next picture confirmed it, as did the next, and the again the next. Anger began to stir as the crystal frame slipped from his hand and shattered on the tile below.

"Undercover! Agent Wilson laughed aloud. "Duh! She was playing under the clown."

The premise allowed the jealous agent to calm down. Until he entered the bedroom that is. The first thing that caught his attention was the huge poster bed that dominated the room.

Wilson couldn't help himself from laying across it. He just wanted to be where she had been. How many times had he fantasized about being in her bed. He scooped up a pillow and inhaled, hoping to catch a whiff of her essence – a sample of the sweet smell that graced the office whenever Demi walked through.

Instead it smelled of men's cologne. He angrily tossed it aside knocking over something on the opposite side of the bed. He went around to investigate and found a tripod and hi-def camera.

Reason told him he didn't want to see whatever was on the camera, but still he connected it to the large plasma screen that took almost the entire wall it was mounted upon.

Wilson sighed a breath of relief and got an instant hard-on as a naked Demi appeared. She was laying in the same bed fingering herself.

"You like that?" Demi asked as she pleasured herself.

"You know I do! You gonna come for me?" A male off screen was heard saying.

"Yes daddy!" She whimpered as she brought herself to a shuddering orgasm.

"Damn! That was good," the man laughed, "guess you don't need me, so I'm finna go."

"Boy stop! You better come fuck me," Demi demanded.

The agent's heart stopped as a naked Cam came into view. He watched in a state of shock as Demi instantly took him into her mouth, After a few minutes of oral sex, Cam fucked his woman vigorously.

The agent hadn't realized he had begun to masturbate until an orgasm was imminent.

"Shit!" He exclaimed looking for something to release himself into. He grabbed a pair of his partner's panties and came just as Cameron did.

Wilson went into the bathroom to clean himself and got another surprise. In the small decorative trash can were three separate positive pregnancy tests.

The agent vowed right then that Cameron Forrest would never be arrested. He was going to kill him himself first chance he got.

CHAPTER
37

I t took some doing but Wilson convinced his superiors to let him go undercover. Even though he grew up in the Bronx, New York, they considered him soft. Wasn't sure if he could pull off posing as a drug dealer.

However, his recent displays of aggression changed their minds. His intel showed that Chris was planning on moving operations to Atlanta. A move that would surely turn bloody.

Agent Wilson's mind snapped in Demi's condo. He wasn't pretending to be a drug dealer, he was one. He was tired of being the nice guy, nice guys finished last.

Here he was tall, fair complexioned, handsome and college educated. Yet the love of his life didn't give him the time of day. Instead she chose a high school dropout, drug dealer.

"Make way for the bad guy," he snarled at his reflection.

He was now dressed in the latest clothes favored by dealers. His platinum and diamond chain was adorned with a diamond 'B', to match his new moniker.

Anthony Wilson was now B-large. Strapped with and endless supply of government money he quickly made inroads into Atlanta's drug world. If one single thing shocked him most it was how much so called thugs talked.

They gave him a wealth of information. Some he shared, some he didn't. The big mouth dealers put him in contact with other big mouth dealers. As a result he was able to make purchases from midlevel dealers.

The more coke he bought, the more he moved up. He had begun to overcharge his employer which allowed him to amass a great deal of cash and coke. It was time to hit the streets.

As any drug dealer will tell you, the money is far more addictive than the drugs themselves. With every dollar B-large made he slipped deeper into character. The line between good guy and bad guy began to blue. There he crossed.

$$***$$

"We got a big problem homie!" Dondi announced wearily. He was B-large's second in command.

Dondi was from Queens, New York and had a little crew of dealers but lacked the resources to move into the big leagues. B-large recruited him and they were now in the majors.

"What's good son?" B-large asked aware of the man's tendency to be dramatic.

"That nigga 'T-Mac' said he ain't paying you, fuck you, and if you don't like it you know where he be," Dondi said in one breath.

"Say Word!" B laughed. "That's what's up."

197

B-large did know where 'T-Mac' was, and that's where the police found his body the next day. He waited for the man and shot him to death without conversation. He then put his own team in the housing project 'T-Mac' once supplied.

It was a bold move. Just the kind of gangsta shit Chris loved. When he got wind of it he knew it was time they met.

CHAPTER

38

C hris move into Atlanta's drug market was easier than expected. He was warned that the Mexicans who controlled the weight distribution might be a problem so he murdered them all. His enforcer Malik killed indiscriminately until they made their point.

Then he began selling bricks of ninety percent pure cocaine for sixteen stacks. He was soon the man. Being the man had its advantages.

Chris bought a mansion in one of the affluent suburbs. That's where he housed his conquest Maria. He had a swank penthouse apartment downtown where he spent most of his time.

The crew was unstoppable. They took over any club they went to. Average dudes walked out as soon as they walked in.

Atlanta is a city full of ballers so it rained in the strip clubs every night. But Chris and company were a hurricane. They turned even upscale clubs into strip clubs. Even sidity chicks came out their business suits when enough money got tossed.

Chris was also a well known freak. It wasn't unheard of for him to solicit a blow job in the VIP. He also had a penchant for young girls. He sought out the ones who wore bands signaling bartenders that they were over 21.

Agent Wilson now known as B-large knew Chris better then he knew his new self. He'd been assigned to him for five years now.

Now that he was a major figure in Atlanta's drug trade it was time to meet his target. He secretly admired the known killer and adapted some of his mannerisms as his own.

"Ayo B, there go them niggas now," Dondi announced to his boss as Chris and company walked in.

"Hurry up ma," B-large demanded the young woman who was under the booth blowing him. To help matters along he grabbed her head and forced her to move faster.

✳✳✳

"Look at this nigga!" Chris laughed as he sat in a booth opposite B-large and entourage. "Who this nigga think he is? Me?"

"Nigga act like you for real son," Malik agreed. He should know. He's spent the last week watching his every move. His surveillance was amateur which allowed B-large to present a carefully prepared image.

"That's the nigga killed T-Mac? Took over the whole projects?" Chris admired. "I love that gangsta shit!"

B-large rapped up by coming in the girl's mouth as he forcefully held her head.

"Un uh take it! Take it!" He demanded the squirming gagging woman.

"What, I'm supposed to go to that nigga?" he asked once he got himself together.

"He's the man right now so yeah we go to them for now," Dondi advised.

Malik stood as B-large and Dondi approached. He and Dondi exchanged pounds and hugs before introducing their bosses.

"Heard a lot about you," B-large announced as they shook hands.

"Anything good?" Chris asked.

"No not really – well product wise yeah," B-large admitted. "Other than that, NO."

"I must be doing something right then," Chris laughed. "I ain't running for office!"

The two drug dealers talked for hours about how to expand Atlanta and then the rest of the east coast.

They agreed upon terms that would allow the agent to make millions. He was becoming less agent by the day. They made more enemies by the day as well.

CHAPTER

39

"Say Shawty, who da fuck are these New York niggas anyway?" Nard demanded. He was hot about getting pushed further out the game everyday.

"First they ran the migos off, then raised the price, and now they won't sell us nothing!" He asked his right hand man J.T.

"Nigga said he will let us work his pack!" J.T. announced. "But won't sell us no weight."

He just tried to purchase some weight from Malik and got chumped off.

"Work they pack! That's what the nigga said?" Nard said getting angrier. "For real! Work his pack!"

"That's what the nigga told me. I started to pull a Cam and murk that nigga," J.T. said.

"A who?" Nard demanded. "Fuck you on that nigga nuts for?"

"Just sayin' Shawty," J.T. said backing down. Nard was a killer and he didn't feel like dying.

"Shit you might be right," Nard admitted. "we beefin' with each other and let some out of town niggas set up shop."

"What we gone do Shawty?" J.T. asked solemnly.

"Nothing," he replied. "For now we wait."

CHAPTER

40

Tywanna talked the entire ride to New York. Cam learned that her addict of a mother sold everything in the house before finally offering her daughter for sale.

He couldn't help but notice she had a striking resemblance to his long deceased mother. Cam knew full well what the streets would do to a pretty young girl and resolved to protect her from it.

"Well, I'm your daddy now," Cam said warmly. "No one will ever hurt you again."

"My daddy?" Tywanna frowned. She had a crush on the handsome man, but was not to be. "OK, ain't never had one of dem. A momma either."

Cam had brought a prepaid phone with internet to replace the one Tywanna left at the hotel. She sent another message on Facebook and halfway through North Carolina they got a response.

"212, must be for you," Tywanna said when the number appeared on the screen.

"Hold on," Cam said when he answered. He pulled the car to the shoulder and got out to speak.

"Ayo who dis?" the voice on the other end demanded.

"This is Cameron Forrest," Cam said defiantly. "Your son!"

"My what! Nigga stop playin' on me," the voice spat before the line went dead.

"Look Shawty! You remember Tywanna Cam said angrily when he called back.

"From Atlanta? Eastwyck?" he questioned, shock evident in his voice.

"Eastwyck! Decatur nigga!" Cam retorted. "That was my momma!"

"Was? Where you at?" Cameron Senior urged.

"75 north, headed your way and I'm hot," Cam said.

"Hot? Yeah you must be related to me," the man laughed.

He gave his newly discovered son an address in the Bronx, New York before getting back to business. His business was smoking crack cocaine.

Cameron Forrest Senior hadn't always been a smoker. In fact, he was once one of the most feared men in all five boroughs. What started as a 'get high' session evolved into a habit. Still he wasn't one of the filthy rundown crack heads. He had a good paying job.

His specialty was wet work. Cam Senior was a hit man. Chris may have been a sociopath but Sr. was a professional.

205

Cam navigated the city streets and found the address his father gave. It was in the Highbridge section of the Bronx. He pulled up in front of the basketball courts and stared at the man smoking a menthol on a bench.

"Is that him?" Tywanna asked pulling Cam out of his thoughts.

"Yeah," Cam replied looking at the older version of himself. "Wait here!"

"Get the fuck outa here!" Cam Sr. laughed as his son approached. "Ayo B you look just like me! I thought you was on some bullshit. I was gonna wet you." He lifted his shirt to reveal the handle of a large automatic.

The men sat down on the bench and began to talk. The conversation started slow then grew to the friendly banter of old friends.

Eventually Cam got around to the shootout that left him homeless and on the run.

"You can stay with me as long as you need," his father advised.

"Won't be long," Cam sneered." I just need a second to regroup. I'm gonna murder Chris and everyone with him."

"I might can help you with that," his dad smiled. Murder was his specialty and this one was personal. His son's beef was his beef. "Who the girl?

"That's my daughter," Cam chuckled. "Her name's Tywanna too."

✳✳✳

Over the next few months Cameron senior instructed his son in the art of war. Young Cam was a killer but his was a war.

When his lessons ended, Tywanna's began. He knew he was fighting a war he could not win. His only objective was to kill Chris before he got killed himself. He wanted to teach her everything he could to survive.

Being a veteran of the dope game, that's where he started. He taught her how to buy coke, judging its quality by sight and taste. Taught her how to cook, cut and bag dope.

Then took her out and taught her to trap. They hit the block at night and sold crack. She complained about the constant standing and cold temperatures but her pleas fell on deaf ears.

"Starving is worse than standing," he shot back. "You rather sell dope or your ass?"

"Dope!" she shot back indignantly. "I ain't never gonna let no nigga buy me."

"Cam smiled inwardly at her defiance. She was a stunning beauty already at 15 so he schooled her on the games men played. What better teacher. Cam was a master.

Still he ha to take notice of how smart she was. You show Tywanna something once and you wouldn't have to show her again. Most times she figured out a way to improve upon it.

"He gave her the streets. His father gave her self defense. All that was left was college. Her adopted father and grandfather urged her to exploit her above average I.Q.

With no other family, the day would come that young Tywanna would be on her own. That day was growing near.

CHAPTER

41

The City of Atlanta and its outlying suburbs were engaged in a nasty turf war. Not only were the locals battling the invaders from New York for the streets, but Mexican hit squads also came into the mix.

The Mexicans also took Chris and his crew to war to control the weight market in the city. Bodies were dropping all over town and something had to give.

Agent Wilson, aka B-large was so deep undercover that he'd stopped reporting to his handlers. Since he was directly involved in the war he was the only one making any money, and lots of it.

Dondi and the rest of the team were able to go where on one else could. Chris and the Mexicans were also involved in a price war that enabled B-large to make millions.

He may have forgotten who he was in all the hype, but he never lost focus of his hatred. B-large knew one day Cam would have to resurface and whenever, of wherever he did, he would be waiting.

After training for six months it was time for Cam to leave. He kept tabs on his target and the war from long distance.

Good thing for him Chris loved the spotlight. Even in the midst of a war, dude still threw lavish parties. He promoted heavily on the radio and internet. The Mexicans had too much to lose to try and strike in public but not Cam. That's exactly how he planned to kill him, publicly.

✲✲✲

"Please, please, please take me with you!" Tywanna pleaded desperately. "I have to stay with you!"

"Not this time sugar," he said wearily. He knew chances of surviving were slim to none. To further protect the girl, he called Mississippi authorities and took responsibility for the hotel clerk murder. She was free.

"Stay here with your granddad and great-grandma. They'll take care of you," Cam said standing to leave. He kissed her on the forehead as tears streamed down her cheeks.

"Please!" she urged grabbing his shirt. "Don't leave me!"

"I have to," he said pulling away. He tossed the numbered bankbooks on the bed and walked out without looking back.

"To hell with you too! You just like everyone else!" Tywanna screamed furiously. "You leave me I ain't going to college! I swear I'ma be just like you! Fuck college! I'ma be a dope girl! You hear me! A Dope Girl!"

CHAPTER

42

"Please, please, please! Take me with you! I have to go with you!" Tywanna pleaded desperately when Cam broke the news to her. His Intel told him that time to move on Chris was now since they were spread thin from the ongoing turf war.

If he gave them a chance to re-group he may never catch him. Still the girls heart wrenching plea had moved him for a split second he thought...

"Not this time sugar" he sighed wearily. He knew the chances of surviving were slim to none, he had to go it alone. It was personal.

"Stay her you're your grand-dad and great–grandma, they'll take care of you" He said standing to leave. He had no doubt that they would since over the past six months they had bonded as a family.

The Forrest family embraced the girl instantly. Likewise, having never had a family Tywanna was able to relax for the first time in her fifteen years on the planet. Did not have to fend for herself or fight off strange men in her own home. She was finally safe.

"Please dont leave me daddy" she begged the man whom she accepted as her father. The words paused him but ultimately he moved on. For some revenge was stronger than love, and when the revenge stems from the loss of loved ones there's no reasoning.

Cam tossed the numbered bank books on the bed and walked out with out looking back. That's when the little girl lost it!

"To hell with you too then! You just like err body else you leaving me too!" Tywanna screamed furiously. "You leave me I aint going to college! I swear I'ma be just like you! Fuck college! I'ma be a dope girl! You hear me, A Dope Girl!"

Cam walked out but stopped in the project hallway stalled by a heavy heart. Tywanna's tirade affected him deeply. Especially the part of him being like everyone else.

Even though it wasn't true the words still echoed in his head. He knew of her abusive upbringing and knew she was alone in the world.

Still, he had to handle his B.I. some people had to die. There would be no more waking up in cold sweats from the night-mares. No more seeing Trisha's dead eyes and Chris toasting her death. No, it was time to kill, even if it meant dying himself. As long as Chris died first Cam didn't mind dying.

"A-yo son glad I didn't miss you" Cam Sr. said rushing out into the hallway. The short sprint had him winded but he still took a furious drag off his menthol.

"Yeah shawty, just taking a second to think" Cam replied. After six months in which he had gotten extremely close to his father Cameron still referred to him as 'shawty', never dad. Cameron senior called him son, but this was New York and everyone called everyone son. Or 'B' no matter you're your name began with.

"That little girl still going off in there" senior said through a plume of gray smoke.

"Lil mama hot!" Cam laughed, "I'ma be a dope girl ya hear me!" The two men laughed at his mocking Tywanna voice and heavy accent,

"You ready to roll son? I'm coming with you" Cam's father announced.

"I got this shawty, like I said, this shit is personal. I'ma murder this nigga Chris and whoever don't like it" He growled.

"Cool, let's ride" senior said leading the way as if he hadn't heard a word he just said.

Not feeling much like debating Cam followed his father out to the car. Both men had little more than a change of clothes and guns. Nothing more was needed since neither expected to be returning.

The car was completely silent as the men began the 13 hour trek south. Both were consumed in their own thoughts until they were halfway through New Jersey,

"Say shawty, why you doing this? Why you coming? "Cam asked his father. "And don't give me that b.s about not being left with them 'chicks' ole man!"

"That's the main reason! my crazy mom and that mean little girl! I'm dead either way!" He joked and laughed. The death statement hung in the air even after the laughter subsided.

"All I want is my man, I don't care much what happens after that" young Cam confessed. It was by no means a death wish but it was the only way to even the score.

He had killed many people on his rise to the top including his own blood. Dying may be the only way to right the wrongs. Besides, dying wasn't so bad. "This nigga Chris is an animal. You aint never dealt with his kind before. A monster!" Dad advised. It was saying a lot coming from the most feared hit man on the eastern seaboard.

"Dude is Freddie, Jason and Osama bin Laden all rolled into one. He'll go where most men wont, where most men cant" Senior continued.

"what about you, can you go there?" Cam asked now happy to have him along.

"Go there? That's where I stay!" He laughed. "Only killer I know worse than me is killa, if he wasn't my nephew I would be afraid of him too!"

Cameron had heard rumors of the man called killa but didn't believe them. He himself had been the target of highly embellished urban legend. Who kills someone and then blows up the funeral home?

"Damn you smoke a lot shawty" Cam complained as his father lit yet another cigarette. "You gone mess around and get cancer."

"Get?, Got!" He admitted through a cloud of smoke. "Stage four, lung and now bone."

214

"Shit shawty" Cam frowned and struggled not to swerve at the bad news. That, of course did explain the death wish. Soldiers hate dying in bed. They wanna go out fighting. Cam junior understood perfectly. He was a soldier too.

"Yeah I found out about a week before yall showed up. Started wilding too! Getting high, fucking all kind of broads raw, tripping!" Dad lamented. "I was tryna speed up the process until you and that girl came along."

"Aight so what we 'posed to do about some burners? We cant take these niggas to war with one 40 cal and a nine" Cam said eager to change the morbid conversation.

"Don't worry I got a guy. He can get us a fucking tank if we need one."

"We may can use it! This one is going down in the history books! The battle for Atlanta!" Cam cheered.

The murderous father and son duo made banal small talk as they continued their journey south. A casual observer would have thought them on a fishing trip. Not off to war. Mid-way through the state of Virginia senior pulled out his phone to call home. "What's good ma?" He said to his sons' amusement New Yorkers called everybody 'ma', even their mothers.

"Yeah we in V.A now" dad said as Cam half listened to the one sided conversation.

He was too busy fondly reflecting on the past six months spent getting to know the father and grandmother he didn't know. Daughter too he smiled at the thought of Tywanna. The girl was a damn trip.

She had made a remarkable transformation during their time together. Even though he had plenty of his own children he had spent more time with her than any of them. He was always in the streets. Since that's what he knew best that's what he taught her.

Hustling is a skill that transfers to any and every occupation. It deals with manufacturing so he taught her to cook coke. Quality assurance. So he taught her how to check the quality of blow by eye, touch and taste. Supply and demand, Market share, etc, etc. Yes, it's a lot more than standing on a corner slinging rocks but he taught her that too.

Also taught her the repercussions of pumping on a corner that's not yours to pump on. A group of young hustlers approached guns drawn one night to confront them. Looking like his father saved his life that night. It was the first time family resemblance saved the day, it would not be the last.

His grandmother Deidra was an interesting mix of the hood and the burbs. An absolute Diva, sophisticated and worldly, yet down home ghetto. For all her degrees, travels and experiences she was still a project chick at heart.

Deidra adored her new found grandson and treated him like a king. Likewise, having never had a daughter of her own she took to Tywanna instantly. The two were thick as theives.

"A-yo son" Cameron said handing the phone to his son, "your grandma"

Cam took the phone with mixed emotions. He had already said his painful, final goodbyes and didn't want to go through it again, Didn't want the sweet old woman to try to talk him out of what had to be done.

She didn't, she fully understood the mechanics of the underworld and that it is what it is.

"Hey grandma" he croaked from emotions. They made congenial small talk about the goings on of the world.

"Just kill who you gotta kill and come on back, ok baby?" She pleaded.

"K mama, let me speak to that girl" he said wanting to comfort Tywanna. It troubled him to have left her so distraught.

Cam could hear a muted dialog in the background before his grandmother came back on the line again.

"She's not ready to talk yet baby, give her some time she's still upset" Deidra said apologetically.

"Ok grandma" Cam agreed even though time was a luxury he didn't have.

"Shorty still hot huh?" Cameron asked taking his phone back.

"Steamed!!" Cam chuckled, "a dope girl you hear me!"

CHAPTER 2

"Shit shawty, shit stay like this I'ma hafta get me a damn job! Nigga gone be flipping fucking burgers out this bitch!" Jap lamented.

"It aint quite that bad shawty" Nard said even though he was feeling the pinch too. The two men had been major drug dealers in Atlanta until Chris came down and disrupted everything.

First because of his beef with Cam he refused to sell anything to anyone from Atlanta. The only people who could eat was those who he fed directly. Then he dropped the prices so low that any renegades wouldn't be able to compete.

He also had the Mexicans so embroiled in the ongoing turf was that they were virtual out of business.

"The hell it Aint!" Jap shot back, "I had to send all the way to Alabama for a brick! Not only did I pay twenty eight for the shit, but its the same shit them New York niggas got, only cut to hell!"

"Yeah that is fucked up" Nard agreed, "If you don't work for them you don't work."

"Just gotta be patient" Nard replied. He knew his rival turned friend was right. The two men had once been enemies until Chris came down. Even with the new allegiances war cost money. Money they didn't have anymore.

"A storm is headed our way. It's gonna come blow all our problems away."

"Fuck kinda storm packing a punch like that?" Jap asked incredulously.

"Hurricane Cam!" Nard smiled knowingly.

***

"Damn that little bitch is fine! A-yo pull over!" Chris demanded as he spotted a girl in the mall parking lot.

"Yo B, she get mad kids yo" Malik protested as he complied.

218

"I aint gonna marry the broad son, look at that ass!"

The young woman saw the Lamborghini approaching and put a little extra sway in her hips. Her small tribe of children came to a halt when the car stopped next to them.

"Yo ma come here" Chris demanded like the boss that he was.

"Don't yall move!" She ordered her two sons, niece and nephew, and made haste to the caller.

"Check it, call me at this number I'm come scoop you later, you aint on your period today are you?" He said handing her his personal card.

"No" she sang eagerly not the least but offended by the crass come-on. On the contrary she was quite flattered. She made her living off of fucking dope boys and this one was obviously major.

She knew it was to her advantage to be as nasty and freaky as possible to earn a top spot on the hit list! All men have a hit list, chicks they can count on to give it up at the drop of a dime. The ones with the best head usually get top honors.

"Aight, Aight that's what's up." Chris nodded taking in the camel toe displayed in her tight shorts. Almost as an after thought he asked "what's ya name ma?"

"Britney" Cams baby mama sang brightly. She turned to collect his children and headed into the mall making sure to switch hard enough to impress the men.

219

"Slow down esse" Poncho warned as Flaco pulled noticeably close to the car they were trailing. It contained Dex and O.C, two of Chris's couriers and a duffle bag full of either coke or money.

"Don't tell me how to trail a car homie I been doing this since you was pissing your pantalones!" Flaco shot back.

"I'm sick of this cat and mouse shit! We're supposed to be at war, but where's the shooting!" Poncho grumbled. Their immediate task at hand was to find stash spots. After they were located they were burned to the ground.

"Rivas said don't move on them so we don't move on them" Flaco replied hotly. He wanted to get into the fray just as much as his trigger happy sidekick.

"What if it aint us?" Ponche smiled as the idea sign flashed above his head. He was a loyal soldier but was bored of the chess game the boss was playing.

For all their surveillance Chris, the main target was rarely spotted. Whenever he did move it was en-masse with security or very public.

"Pull right up next to it" Ponche said chambering a round in the calico sub-machine gun on his lap. It had a hundred round drum and Poncho intended to empty it.

Flaco pulled along side of the car and honked the horn. It took a few more burst of the horn before the wreckless drug couriers heard it over the blaring music.

"See what them 'wet backs' want" Dex ordered from the passenger side. O.C began to let down the window as Poncho Lifted the gun.

The first few rounds of semi-automatic gun fire took O.C's entire forehead off causing the car to slam into a telephone pole. If they have cars in the afterlife I bet Dex will wear his seat belt because not wearing it cost him this life.

His head slammed into the dashboard and dazed him. The few seconds it took to shake it off were too many. Poncho was by his door when he opened it and opened fire. He was going to have to have one of those funerals where they have the picture of you by the casket because the black talon rounds gave him a face lift. Lifted his face to roof of the car.

"Take the bag!" Flaco reminded. This would make it a robbery and shift the blame away from the Mexicans. Every time they bumped heads with the blacks they only took lives, never money of drugs.

Now Chris would think it was the Atlanta faction that did the hit, then he would hit back. Which was what he wanted to do all along.

***

"Bad news boss" Malik sighed, his face wore a mask of remorse that hid his true feelings. He was ecstatic someone finally set it off. He was a murderer and wanted to murder something.

"What now?" Chris snapped. He was already in a foul mood after checking his numbers. This Atlanta move was personal, not business and as such was failing. Between loosing product and men he was operating at a loss by reducing prices to shut out competitors.

"Dex and O.C got hit, they're both dead" Malik said suppressing a smile. He didn't understand how the dumb asses made it this long. They should have been dead. "They had a hundred k and ten bricks"

"The Mexicans took money? They never take our money" Chris questioned.

"Had to be them country nigga's! They tried us! Tried you!" Malik instigated, he knew it didn't take much to whip the mad man into a murderous frenzy.

"Say word! Them niggas think it's a game! They take me a joke!" Chris said taking the bait. "They want it like that? Bet, kill them all! Kill everybody!"

The ego maniac had effectively put a hit on the whole city. It was a war he could not win. He was a beast, no question, but he had now officially bitten off more than he could chew. This was the pride before the fall.

CHAPTER

43

"Turn right" The navigation announced in signaling the end of their journey. Cam took a deep breath and exhaled a stress filled sigh. It was a gesture one makes when they are about to do something they really don't want to do but has to.

"A-yo son you sure you can trust these dudes?" Cameron asked his son as he pulled off the main road onto a long wooded drive. "The enemy of your enemy isn't always your friend"

"Well, two things" the younger killer began. "First we share a common goal. It's to all of our benefit to kill them niggas! And two, too late now."

As the last word left Cams mouth gunmen holding AK-47 assault riffles stepped out from several directions, at the same time Nard stepped out onto the porch.

"Easy dad" Cam said as his father gripped his pistol. "Them choppers will cut us in half 'fo you let off one shot"

"A-yo son, you called me dad!" Senior gushed proudly. "No I didn't shawty" Cam shot back embarrassed. "Yeah you did" His father laughed.

Nard and the gunmen looked on curiously as the two had a friendly argument, finally Nard shrugged and approached.

"Um... excuse me?" He said tapping on the driver side window.

"One second shawty" Cam said, then turned back to stress his point some more. Nard could only laugh and head back inside.

Once the father and son agreed to disagree they opened their doors to head inside.

"Hold up shawty, we gotta check yall" one of the men said. He passed off his chopper to another and stepped forward to conduct the search.

"Here" Cam said handing over his gun. The man then turned to senior with a hand extended.

"Fuck outa here yo! I'm not giving you my hammer!" He chuckled. "Yall cats strapped, I'm keeping mine too!"

Not knowing what to do or say he let him keep it. They walked up the steps and into the house where Nard and company awaited.

"Welcome shawty, we've been waiting on you. The whole city been waiting on you" Nard smiled.

"Here I am!" Cam said taking his place with the rest of Atlanta's drug lords. All in attendance were stars in the underworld but they all respected Cam. He was the 'Dope Boy', books would one day be written about him.

Just as scones and cocktails are served in country clubs the ghetto celebrities passed around blunts of kush and sipped cognac.

"This nigga is like the invisible man" Nard complained through a fog of dense weed smoke. "He everywhere and no where at the same time."

"That cat will rent out the whole club when he wants to party" Jap added. "He even bought the whole plaza where his girl has a beauty parlor"

"Shit that's easy! We can find out what club he's gonna be in and just blow the shit up!" Cameron senior suggested.

All in attendance snapped their heads in his direction upon hearing the unusually violent plan. These were all violent men, killers, but blow up a whole club!

"Allow me to introduce Cameron Forrest, my father" Cam said proudly.

"Only way to get next to that nigga is if you got a pussy. All he do is fuck young broads all day" Jay spoke up.

The Trap stars nodded in agreement knowing it was indeed the best way. They all could have got caught slipping behind a woman. Most had eliminated an enemy or two in that manner.

Pussy, or the pursuit of pussy had been the down fall of many great men. An erection was like an Achilles heel, kryptonite to common sense.

That's why they all kept young ruthless chicks on their teams. A plan was hatched to sic the young girls on the pussy hound. As one hundred thousand dollars bounty was pledged for whatever girl could get a location on him.

"Just get him anywhere for five minutes and leave it up to me" senior announced before a violent coughing spell wracked his body.

"You ok shawty, need some water?' one of the killers asked compassionatley.

"Water for cancer?" Dad laughed regaining his composure. The show of weakness cut him to the core.

Once the plan was hatched and the blunts burned out Cam and his father stood to leave. They all exchange pounds and hugs before dispatching,

"So what cha think?" Cam asked his father once they reached the main road.

"I think that main one is gonna try you the second after you kill Chris" he replied matter factly.

"Yeah me too" Cam laughed "That's if I don't get him first! Besides the nigga who kills me only gonna be famous for a minute cuz he coming right behind me. The city loves me shawty!"

"A-yo what's up with the Rachets? A nigga can stand a little tightening up, feel me?" Dad asked eagerly.

"You sure you up to that?"

"Look uh … shawty. I got lung cancer, aint shit wrong with my dick!" Dad shot back.

226

"Shit as a matter fact I do, I gotta mother, daughter we can hit. I gotta stop by anyway" Cam said grinning. "Ain't no heat over there, we might be able to hide out there".

"Let me guess, I get the mother?"

"I'll take the mother with her freaky ass! The daughter straight but mom!" Cam explained."The pussy better that a government check!"

"Ok, ok I'll take the mom!" Dad laughed.

CHAPTER

44

"Any word from our esteemed colleague?" Special agent Fitz asked agent Ford upon catching him alone in a hallway. It was beginning to look as if the agent had actually gone rogue.

It wouldn't be the first time an undercover agent had slipped into the other side. In fact it happened a lot. A lot more than the agency wanted to admit. Just recently a white female agent infiltrated a major Meth operation. Within months she was a full fledged addict. She actually fought against her own team when they swooped in to make arrest. Of course it was played in the media that she was killed by the dealers. That meant the agents on the scene had to kill the two dealers who gave up as well. This case could not go to trial.

Nelson Ford and Anthony Wilson AKA B-large had once been close, but as the latter slipped further into character the two had become estranged. Agent Ford was now secretly assigned to him as a support.

"Nothing out of the ordinary" he lied. His investigation into his former friend put him into millionaire status. The sixty grand a week he turned in was a drop in the bucket.

"He is close to the main target Christopher Barnes, he is buying kilos directly from him. We are close to an arrest."

"Things are getting bloody on the streets. This war has escalated. I want it wrapped, NOW!" The boss demanded. "A.S.A.F.P!"

"Yes sir" Ford replied eagerly. After all he was ready to make his play. He saw how big the pie was and wanted his slice.

***

"A-yo, where the fuck is this nigga Dondi at?" B-large barked. He hadn't heard from his right hand man and second in command in days.

"Beats the hell out of me" Elijah replied. "I been calling, voice mail was full, now it going straight to voice mail. Aint nobody heard from him since he went to make a buy from Malik".

"I want you to personally go to his house and drag his ass in here!" B-large demanded hotly. It was a front, in truth he was worried about the man. They had been close, but his demeanor had been off as of late.

Elijah took off like a shot to complete his task. In his heart he hoped the man had run off with either the dope or money. That would mean a promotion for him. As he raced toward Stone Mountain he tried Dondi's phone every few minutes.

Even as he pulled behind his truck in the driveway there was no answer.

"Say shawty! A-yo!" Elijah called out as he rang the bell. He began pounding on it once he got no reply.

With no luck at the front door he tried the side, it too was locked tight and went unanswered. He went around back knocking and looking in windows as he went.

Kitchen: nothing, living room: nothing, den: nothing, office: Dondi stretched out with a huge hole in the top of his head. A pool of blood had turned black and a million flies played and reproduced in the brain matter that fell out the hole.

"Fuck!" Elijah grimaced as he pried open the window and got a nose full of the putrid aroma of dead flesh. The smell had knocked him back several feet but the open satchel full of cash urged him on.

Elijah retreated to his car and doused a handkerchief with scented oil that he copped from the Muslims over in the west end. He also dumped the contents of his gym bag to tote the cash. He knew the smell of death had to be embedded the bag it was in. Mind you this is the same man who rode around with a dead man in his trunk for a week.

The oil had provided some relief from the smell but Elijah still wretched from the odor. He fought not to vomit because that would mean him having to burn the entire house down to erase his D.N.A.

"No you didn't!" He laughed upon seeing the murder weapon still clutched tightly in Dondi's dead hand. It was obvious from the carnage that his former associate had inserted the forty caliber pistol into his mouth and blew the top of his head off. A second plot formulated in the trechous mans mind and he acted.

"Let it go" Elijah grunted as he pried the gun from his hands. The note explaining why the seemingly happy man took his own like went in after it. Elijah didn't read one word. Didn't care. Now the world would never know why the seemingly happy husband and father took his own life. We just have to deal with it.

"Boss, you're not going to believe this!" Elijah proclaimed when B-large came on the line. He was right too, because the boss instantly became suspicious.

Most times when people say 'you're not going to believe this' or 'I'ma tell you the truth', they are lying.

"What aint I gonna believe?"" B-large demanded, already twisting his mouth up like 'yeah right'.

"Dondi is dead! I just left there, aint no money or drugs no where!" He said glancing at the bag of money on the back seat. He winced from the smell of it and planned to wash it as soon as he got it home. It put a new spin on the term laundry money.

"What happened? How?" B-large asked slumping into a chair. He had become fond of the man and took the death hard.

"I aint for sure, but I asked around and a kid told me he heard shots a couple of days ago and saw a red vette speed away." He replied putting the murder on Chris Barnes right hand man Malik. Malik was the proud owner of a red Corvette.

"Malik?" The agent blurted in disbelief. "Why in the world would Malik kill Dondi?"

"The money, why else?" Elijah smiled.

CHAPTER

45

"Tywanna! Girl I know you hear me" Grandma Deidra moaned as she stuck her head in the girls room.

"I'm not Tywanna anymore" she said back with a smile.

"Lawd! Who are you now? Wait, that's right you're the Dope girl!" she teased and cracked up. They had all gotten a kick out of her tirade even her. She laughed along even though she was serious. That street shit amazed the girl, she loved it.

"No, my name is Cameisha! C.A.M.E.I.S.H.A!" She spelled out.

"Well ok ms. C.A.M.E.I.S.H.A!" get dressed so we can G.O." grandma chuckled.

"I was thinking about that too" Camelisha said with a nod. "I'm not sure that's a good idea. Perhaps I should just stay home with you".

"Girl your going to school! No choice there. Now if you want some new clothes to go in I suggest you get dressed now" Deidra said firmly.

"Yes ma'am" The obedient girl replied. She adored her adopted grandmother and was eager to please her. If going to school was going to make her happy then she would do it. Now matter how much she hated it.

All eyes were on the two as they walked through the projects court yard to catch a cab. A group of girls stared at Cameisha so she stared back. She had been taught a lot of things during her stay in New York but fear was not one of them.

"Grandma, I think I'ma hafta fight one dem gals" Cameisha said snarling at the group. Her southern accent always got more pronounced when she was upset.

Deidra looked over at the group of mismatched misfits and shook her head. Not only did she know the trifling pack of girls she knew they weren't shit. She know their mothers and grandmothers and they weren't shit either.

"Don't be naïve girl" she replied with a huff. "You're gonna have to fight all them girls!"

"Un uh grandma, just one" Cameisha said staring at the leader. She had been down this road before with Big Bessie back home.

"That bitch swear she cute!" Crystalline barked to her flunkies.

"She is cute!" Aqua blurted out without thinking, something she did a lot of and stayed in trouble because of it.

"No she aint" Zaria said coming to the aid of their ugly leader.

Crystalline looked like an x-men mutant. She had big heavy brows and wide face and one of her eyes had a mind of its own.

To compensate she over compensated with wigs, weaves, eye lashes and other accessories that only made her look comical. Strangers often laughed upon seeing her for the first time until they realize she was serious.

Crystalline was as mean as she was ugly and thoroughly dominated her pack. Zaria was beautiful but smart enough to play down her looks around her friends. Dressing down to appease the girl. She just got cute at home.

Aqua too was cute but dumb as dirt. Her low IQ classified her as mildly retarded but that didn't matter in the projects. After her third abortion by age 13 her mother had her spayed and neutered.

Dasia and Angle, yes Angle. Her mother meant Angel but couldn't spell it. Everyone except the teachers at school called her Angel. They rounded out the crew of rachet girls. They terrorized the pretty girls for being pretty and regularly jumped them.

A sign reading 'will fuck for blunts' was once etched into the bench that served as their hang out, but it had been worn off. No matter the hood knew and the young dealers would take breaks to knock them off in the pissy stairs wells.

"Bitch you wanna go hang out with them!" Crystalline barked. "Matter fact get yo ass over there with them!"

Aqua got up and hung her head prepared to follow as told. She did what she was told faithfully. Be it steal, cheat, lie, fuck, whatever.

"Sit yo dumb ass down!" Crystalline next demanded.

"Guess we may as will step to them first" Grandma Deidra suggested.

"No grandma!" Cameisha laughed assuming the woman was joking. She wasn't. "This my fight, I'll take care of this"

"Ok yall bitches know who grandmother that is!" Sincerity warned as she passed by. None of the crew appreciated being called bitches even though they referred to themselves and each other as such on a daily basis. Of course no one complained either cuz the word stung a whole lot less than Sincerity whooping their ass.

Sincerity was the project fly girl and they did not want a problem with her. She once dated legend, turned myth who went by the name killa. Her only son was named Xavier which only added to the speculations.

"I don't give a fuck who grandma that is" Crystalline whispered even though the hood diva was out of earshot. She was lying, she cared.

✳✳✳

Deidra had a ball shopping for a girl for the first time in her long life. She especially liked that Cameisha loathed all things tight, or short, She had so long been targeted for her good looks that she tried to hide it.

"How about this grandma?" Cameisha said bursting excitedly from the dressing room. She did a twirl so the long flowered dress flowed fluidly.

"It's very nice." Deidre lied. She hated the 'little house on the prairie' style and cut. Not to mention she knew that the pretty girl with the southern accent in a new school was gonna have to fight everyday, she needed pants.

"You can wear it to church or when ever you go back in time" Grandma laughed, "Lets get you some jeans, and boots!"

"Ok grandma, Long as they aint tight", she said fearfully.

"I know baby, I know" Deidra comforted. She had yet to get all the details but could clearly recognize the abuse.

Chapter 6

Britney was giving Chris a live porno show as she rode him backwards. She made sure to rise up the full length of his shaft then make a circle with her ass and slide slowly back down. It was antics like this that got her moved high on the hit list. She was in the starting five.

Business was still business and business was slow so when Chris's phone rang he answered it. Not to mention he was on the verge of busting another quick nut and that was getting embarrassing. Seeing it was B-large he didn't hesitate because they needed to talk.

"Yo what's good fam?" Chris said easily still enjoying the sight and feel of the young cow girl.

"You tell me yo, what is good?" B-large shot back. He was already hot but hearing the moans of the girl made it worse. Here he was calling on a matter of life and death and this nigga was fucking some broad. No respect!

"Nothing you need to tell me?" B-large asked straining not to lose his composure.

"Like what fam? I do need to talk to you about... A-yo hold up!" Chris said urgently as he tapped Britney's ass with his free hand. She knew what it meant and scrambled to get him inside of her mouth.

"Mmm, shit!" Chris moaned as they practiced their version of birth control. It was 100% effective. No one has ever gotten pregnant by swallowing cum.

While on hold B-large faded back to agent Wilson. He finally remembered he was actually law enforcement and not a criminal. He hit the recorder just as Chris finished painting the girl tonsils.

"Ok, you where saying?" Chris laughed only further enraging him.

"I was saying... what happened with my man Dondi? Last I heard he was meeting Malik Furqan to purchase ten kilos of cocaine " The agent said hoping to get talk of both murder and dealing on tape.

"How the fuck am I supposed to know?" Chris barked getting agitated himself now. "I can barely keep up with my own people how the fuck am I supposed to keep track of yours? And speaking of your people, I thought you was supposed to be handling the locals. I got my hands full with these fucking amigos and you let these ATL niggas rob my men!"

"What the hell are you talking about? The locals are on ice" agent Wilson asked puzzled. He knew because he had just gotten off the line with Nard.

"Two of my drivers got hit, they took my blow, ten bricks" Chris replied. "The Mexicans never took anything"

"I'll look into it. Say,I need to double my order since my man skipped on me with my dough" agent Wilson said as a plot formulated. He had an opportunity to kill two birds with one shot.

"Hell yeah!" Chris said eagerly. Business had been so slow he would love twenty kilo sale. "Check, my party is this weekend. Fall through we'll have a few drinks and talk it out."

"See you then!" Wilson said and rushed off the line. He scrambled to turn off the recording for the next call. No sense in getting himself indicted for murder.

"Nard tell your boy Saturday at the hip-hop café." He said and quickly hung up.

"Damn daddy!" Cam laughed at the sounds of vigorous sex echoing in the otherwise quiet house. His father and Mrs. Thompson were getting along famously. They fucked several times a day like teenagers. Cam however, wasn't getting much himself.

Britney was out most nights sexing Chris leaving Cam alone with his children and thoughts. When she did come home she treated him to a blow job before crashing. Being a side piece was a lot of work.

Cam was deep in thought when Britney walked in rambling. He was deep in her throat before he really noticed her. She was going on and on giddily about finally being invited out with the entourage. Even as she blew him she pulled him out of her mouth at frustrating intervals to talk.

Cam was on the verge of politely asking her to please shut the fuck up when he caught on to what she was rambling about. This Chris she was gushing about was the same man he was hunting.

"You mean Chris from New York? Light skin pretty nigga with good hair?"

"Mm hm" she nodded with her head full of dick. She even managed a smile.

He cleverly goaded all the details out of her about the party she was going to miss. He had his man.

✳✳✳

"You OK?" Cam asked, glancing over at his father in the passenger seat.

"Yeah why!" Senior snapped between coughs. The proud man hated feeling vulnerable, hated dying slowly. That was torture for a soldier. He was supposed to die in the heat of battle, an honorable death. Cut down in a blaze of glory taking as many of his enemies with him as possible.

"I was just worried Britney's mom was gonna fuck you to death" Cam said switching gears.

"She might just! That woman is insatiable!" Cameron laughed, "Yo she fucks me in my sleep! Woke up and she was riding my piss hard on!"

"I spoke with grandma last night" Cam offered stoically. "She asked about you but you was screaming 'whose pussy is this!' and what was all the clapping about?"

"Yo she likes me to slap that ass. I gave that fat ass a round of applause!" dad laughed. "So what's up with my granddaughter?"

"Damn girl still won't talk to me" Cam replied with the sting of the snub evident on his handsome face.

"A-yo Shorty is a damn trip!" dad laughed fondly. "I um....I have a confession"

"Oh lawd!" Cam laughed, "What the world could the most dangerous hit man on the east coast have to confess about?"

"Well, um.....I'm saying.....um, OK you know how you use to take little mama out at night teaching her how to hustle?"

"Do I! That girl is a natural! She can weigh by eye, and her whip game is incredible! Better than mine" Cam raved.

"Well once y'all came in and you went to sleep, I took her out and....trained her" dad said sheepishly.

"Trained her what?" Cam asked fearfully.

"To kill" he replied bluntly, "like you said she's a natural. The girl can fight, shoot and stab with the best of them. Her cute little ass giggled when she mastered how to snap a person's neck. I'm afraid she's gonna kill some one!"

"Already has" Cam replied shaking his head solemnly.

"Say word! When? Up in New York? "

"Mississippi, when I first met her. She saved my ass shawty" Cam said reflecting back to the day she came into his life.

"It was right after I had to So-called shoot out with the Feds. Truth be told I didn't get off one shot. Me and my man Went out the side window, smack dab in front of two agents. One was my girlfriend, my pregnant girlfriend. My dude Yu gets off first and... He killed them both, took two to the chest doing it. He saved my life too." Cam stopped talking as the faces of the deceased floated past his eyes. He was the cause of so much death and destruction.

"Anyway, I got out of there and headed west. I drove until I couldn't keep my eyes open anymore, checked into a little motel to crash out. The next morning I woke up all on the news like public enemy number one. Armed and dangerous, kill on sight bullshit. Old man at the motel keeps staring at me like he recognized me but I didn't take heed to it. I should have.

I had nowhere to go and no one to trust that's when I decided to try to contact you. So I go to the library to use the computer but I didn't know shit about social media. I know all the porn sites though! There's this one site! anyway. I see little mama working like she knew what she was doing so I ask her to look you up. She is the one who found you. She charged me lunch for her help, poor thing I could hear her stomach growling. She's going on and on about some kind of special burger as we're leaving and some big Green Mile looking nigga runs up talk about he bought her!"

"Bought!" Senor boomed hotly. He was extremely fond of the little girl he called his granddaughter.

242

"I know, that's why I couldn't leave her. I tried to talk to dude but he slapped the shit outta me!" Cam laughed. "You know I had to two piece him. Put that ass to sleep like MJ's doctor. Now I'm like fuck! I gotta get out of here. I jet to the car and shawty in it before me!

Once we get back to the hotel I send her for that special burger that does back flips or some shit and was going to leave her. I gave her a 100 dollar bill to get her plus keep the change so she could have a few bucks in her pocket. I'm in the shower when I hear the front door open back up and I thought it was little mama but it's the hotel clerk. Dude has a shotgun on me talking about turning me in. I planned to make a try for my gun but it's gone!

That's when Tywanna comes back in and she's got my burner. She took one look at dude and bust! Took the top of his shit off! I ran out of that room in nothing but a towel and again shawty beats me to the ride!

Once we get on the highway she finally asked was he dead. I told her yeah and she laughs, laugh's! Then, starts crying. So I'm tryna comfort her like, 'you had to do it, it was him or me, blah blah blah', she's like, that's not why I'm crying. I'm crying cuz.....wait, hold up" Cam says checking his vibrating cell phone.

"Sup shawty, any luck on our man?" Cam asked upon answering.

"Naw shawty, we still ain't seen that nigga" Nard replied. "But check, we having a little 'thing' this weekend at the hip hop cafe. Rented the whole spot. Come on and hang out".

"Sho-nuff? OK man, I'ma fall through shawty" Cam said woefully then hung up.

"What's the matter son?" Cameron asked his obviously troubled son.

"A wise man once said the enemy of my enemy isn't always my friend". Cam sighed. "Dude just invited me to my murder. And I'm going!"

"I'm coming too!" Senor snarled protectively.

"So what's up with this gun connect of yours we going to meet?" Cam asked primarily to change the subject.

"Who Bigs! That's my mans and dem! "

CHAPTER

46

"Our primary subject Christopher Barnes will sell us 20 kilos of pure cocaine on Saturday night" agent Wilson announced as he briefed his fellow agents. "Also expected at this meeting is Cameron Forrest".

A hush fell over the room as Cams picture came onto the screen. He was the suspect in the death of five of their own. Every man and woman in the room with much rather put a bullet in his head than cuffs on his wrist.

"The logistics of the venue are a Nightmare" Wilson said pulling up diagram of the club. His new blueprints didn't include the passage from the store next door that was built during construction. "One way in, one way out......"

Agent in charge Fitz looked on in Pride and relief that his agent came through. He had been worried that he was in too deep, past the point of no return. Not only did he set up the deal that will put the notorious Christopher Barnes away for life but let his friend and fellow agent head the bust. He was a true team player.

Truth was agent Ford confronted him about his receipts verses his own calculations and demanded his cut. He figured a half mil would keep him quiet for a while. However B-Large had a plan that would keep him quiet for a lot longer for a lot cheaper. No one in that back office was coming out alive. He knew once all those wanted men got together with law enforcement all hell would break loose. There would be no surrender. Once agents breached that office the dealers wouldn't go down without a fight. Dying was part of the game.

Agent Wilson promised Nard the entire city once Chris and Cam were both dead. That too was a lie. He planned to eliminate all the competition in one foul swoop. Then he would go back to work at the agency and protect his drug ring from there.

"You Won't need that" Cameron told his son as he chambered a round in his pistol "this is my man".

"No gun? At the gun buy!" Cam questions as they parked at the gun dealers apartment. The question was rhetorical because he trusted his father implicitly. It's rare to have people in his life that he could say that about. A coughing spell stopped senior dead in his tracks as a son looked on helplessly. A minute later it subsided and he resumed his proud gait.

"Cameron Forrest!" Big Shawn smiled as he opened his door to a long time friend. He opened his wide arm span and embraced him warmly.

"This is my....."

"Son!" Bigs interjected, "looks like you spit him out!" Father and son tried and failed to suppress smiles at the comment that you so often hear. They followed him into the

246

living room and took a seat. That's when Big Shawn's face changed. All of a sudden he look terrified.

"A-yo, your nephew came to visit me last night!" He announced wide eyed. "Just showed up in my bedroom I still don't know how he got in."

"What did he say? What did he want?" Cameron asked eagerly as his son looked on puzzled. He wondered why everyone spoke in hushed tones when it came to the man he doubted even existed.

"Guns, what else? Bigs replied. "Left With enough small arms to start a revolution, paid cash for everything."

"Does he know I'm down here? Senior asked hopefully.

"Didn't Say if he did or didn't. You know he lives in the shadows."

"Well of course you know I need some heat too. Only I ain't got no cash, look at it as a going away present". Cameron said filling the room with the gloom of death. "You got that thing I asked for?"

"Samson? Yeah I got it but..." a coughing spell interrupted his question before he got to finish. "Let's go into the other room let me show you what I got!"

"Fuck!" young Cam exclaimed as they entered the show room full of guns. He had the same look of glee as a child would upon entering a toy store. "My dick just got hard!"

Dad just laughed but he had a stiffy to at the sight of the exotic weapons. "It's going to be an in close firefight" senior said picking up a machine pistol. "A couple of these should get it."

"I got some extended clips for those but still that shit will be empty in under a second!" Bigs warned as Cam fondled an H&K MP5 sub-machine gun.

"A second is all I need" dad said ominously.

"I guess one of these will do me fine" junior said settling on the Heckler and Koch. A Berretta nine mil was picked as a side piece. A bullet proof vest caught his eye but was quickly dismissed. Living past Saturday meant life in prison or life on the run. Neither option suited his taste, his father was right legends go out with a bang. He refused to go out like Saddam Hussein and get caught hiding in a hole in the ground. Only to let his enemies have a way with him and kill him anyway.

"Here is what you asked for" Bigs said solemnly. A sad smile appeared on Camerons face as he inspected the device. The room had gone quiet as the deadly apparatus stole the show. It completed the order so the men then retreated back to the living room.

The two old friends reminisced fondly over past murders. Cam could only shake his head as every subject began with 'remember that dude we killed'. Blunts of Purp helped the stories flow smoothly even through occasional pause for Cam SR to cough.

No one asked him if he was alright because they knew he wasn't. Instead they waited for him to regain his composure and then continued on as if nothing had happened. With heavy hearts the friends embraced tightly. They knew this would be the last time we saw each other in this life. Today was Friday, tomorrow Saturday, there would be no Sunday.

Father and son rode in silence each deep in thought. Half way back to the house Cam finally asked what was on his mind.

"Say shaw...eh pops, what's up with that thing?"

"What, Samson?, it's from the Bible" he began as Cam frowned. He couldn't imagine what Bible contained something like that. "In the Bible we find the story of Samson. A warrior, mad strong and brave. He was beefing with the Philippinos and parasites......"

Cam fought not to laugh at the distorted Biblical passages seeing that his father was serious.

"So when they caught him down bad and was about to body him he used the last bit of his strength to knock the pillars down collapsing the building. It cost him his life too but at least he took them with him. Not to mention he was at the end of his life anyway".

Cam let it soak in as he reflected on his own life. He wasn't terminally ill but with death penalty cases in two states plus the feds he was literally a dead man walking.

What a life it was though! He rose to the top of his chosen profession. How many doctors or even athletes can say that? At least he wore the crown, at least he was the King. Dope Boy for real!

"So what's the plan, run in and kill everyone?" dad asked breaking the silence "cowboy style!"

"Pretty much" Cam nodded, "once I get in that back room I'm gonna murder everything moving! I just need you to hold me down from the front, make sure no one gets the drop on me"

"Bet! I can handle that son" Cameron lied. Picture him playing look out, he had another plan.

✳✳✳

"Hey grandma", Cam said cheerfully when his grandmother came on the line. This was the last of his goodbye calls. He already snuck around to his other kids and grandmother in Atlanta. The two spoke cordially even though the wise woman heard the finality in his voice. Finally Cam asked to speak to 'that girl'.

"Let me see if she'll come..'Cameisha! Your father is on the phone...... Girl I know you better come get this phone!' here she comes now baby. I love you".

"Love you too grandma" he replied as a warm tear trickled down his face.

"Hello" Cameisha said trying to be sassy and failing. Truth be told her heart ached at her father leaving her. She tried the mask the pain with anger, but anger doesn't make you cry at night. That's pain, the pain of a broken heart.

"Hey Tywan....."

"My name ain't Tywanna! It's Cameisha!" she said rolling her neck.

"My bad, I forgot" Cam chuckled. In his mind he could see the head movement. "Look I know you're upset with me, but I gotta do what I gotta do. You have a choice, a future, don't fuck it up, don't be like me. Go to school and get your

250

diploma. Then college, no more 'dope girl'. What I taught you in them streets is transferable to any career".

"OK daddy" she smiled at the mention of her 'dope girl' tantrum. "I'm going to college, but I'm still gonna be a dope girl. A dope girl doctor or lawyer!"

"Now that's what's up!" Cam said proudly. The father and daughter spoke into the wee hours of the morning before finally saying their goodbyes.

CHAPTER

47

Not a particularly religious man Cam spent his last day deep in some pussy. He had settling for blow jobs but now Britney gave it up completely. He wanted to go out with a bang. So did his father judging by the screams coming from down the hall.

"Argh!" Cam grunted as he filled a condom and slumped over Britney's pretty ass. He took a few more innocuous strokes for GP. He lay there until her soft snores could be heard then quietly set off for the shower.

He rushed to wash the sex off him so he could sneak off without his father. His last days would be better spent safe and warm up inside Mrs. Thompson.

"Well, let's go kill some bad guys" Cam told his handsome reflection as he dried off. Having done his job properly Britney was snoring loudly when he crept back into the room. He moved as quietly as possible so not to wake her up. This is one party she needed to miss. The liquor, weed and dick put her to sleep like a baby meaning she will be safe and sound with all the shooting started. He grabbed his guns and crept out of the quiet house.

"The fuck?" Cam questioned at the empty spot that his car should have been in. Who would steal the plain sedan with Mrs. Thompson Benz a few feet away. He marched back in inside the house to get the keys puzzled.

"I need your keys!" He demanded upon finding the exhausted woman in the kitchen guzzling orange juice. "You can pick your car up later, it will be on the news"

"He took them too" she said sobbing silently.

"Who?" Cam asked confused.

"Your father, he took my keys and left."

"Did he say where he was going?" he asked hoping it was only to the store for more menthols or whipped cream with his freaky ass.

"He said he was most likely going to hell" she weeped.

"Did He have that thing on? Samson?" he asked as it all began to come together.

"Lord yes! Even while we Fu.... He wouldn't take it off". Cam suppressed a smile at the thought of his father sexing the sexy woman wearing 'Samson'. He hugged her one last time and rushed out.

Being a true veteran of the hood he knew how to hotwire a car. It wasn't until he twisted the stripped wires together and cranked the engine that he noticed the flat tires. Plan C went out the window as well when he saw Britney's car had suffered the same fate as her mother's. It's sat low to the ground on four flats of its own.

"Sup shawty?" Cam asked defeated as his father answered his phone.

"Chilling son, bout to handle that B.I. for you" senior replied driving towards downtown Atlanta.

"It's my beef, you should let me handle it" Cam said despite the obvious futility.

"I got this son. I missed your whole life the least I can do to try to extend it. I just let the air out of the tires so once you fill them up you're good to go. You have a new lease on life, go live".

"Okay daddy, I love you man" Cam said as he felt an odd sensation trickling down his face. He caught the loan tear as it dropped and stared at it. He had shed more tears in last 24 hour than in his entire life.

"I love you too son" Cameron said through his own tears and hung up.

***

"I want agents here, here, and here!" agent Wilson barked as he set up the mobile command center. He was running the show from the fully equipped van while agent Ford ran the take down squad. "These are your main targets" Wilson Briefed showing a dated picture of Cam as well as recent shots of Chris, Malik and the rest of his lieutenants.

Cameron Forrest senior parked a block away from the venue. He planned to use the same entrance as his son had laid out to get into the club undetected. A severe coughing spell stalls his approach. It's the worst one yet as one of his cancer ravaged lungs fails completely. He staggers on valiantly, wheezing with every strained breath. Using the acquired key to the back door of the adjacent store he slipped inside.

"I just got a visual on subject Cameron Forest!" an agent whispered excitedly into his radio.

Agent Wilson quickly cued up the camera monitoring the back entrance and squinted, "is that him?"

"Looks like" the agent replied just as two of Chris's guards followed senior in. The distinctive 'brrrr' of a fully automatic pistol sent the guards staggering back out. "He fired on the guards!"

"Move, move, move! everybody go!" Wilson screamed starting the raid.

Chris, Malik and Elijah, who B-large sent to transact the doomed deal drew their weapons as senior stumbled into the back office. The men then lowered them at the sight of the hacking older man.

"A-yo who the fuck is you?" Chris demanded looking at that coughing man.

"I'm... I'm.. My son sent me" Cameron announced when he regained his composure. "I came bearing gifts."

Both men eyes grew as wide as dinner plates as Cameron opened his coat and Samson came into view. "What the fuck is that?!" Elijah asked.

"Meet Sampson" Cameron replied pressing in the detonator switched arming the device. "It's 40 pounds of plastic explosives. Once my finger comes off this button, it's off to see the wizard!"

"What the hell is that!?" Chris questioned as the sound of agents battling his security forces reached him. Before anyone had a chance to reply the door came off the hinges and in rushed masked men with guns and badges.

"Put your hands in the air!" agent Ford screamed from behind the sub machine gun. All complied even dad still holding the button. The criminals breathed a sigh of relief as agents filled the room. They would much rather take their chances in the corrupt legal system than with Samson.

"You!" agent Ford barked to senior, "Drop that!"

"OK, if you say so" Cameron Forrest senior smiled and complied.

"What the hell was that" an agent asked as the violent explosion shook the ground under the van.

"I don't know" Wilson lied smiling internally. He knew full well the weight, type, and country of origin of the C 4 he just heard, he was an expert. He also knew what the sound meant the end of all his problems and competition.

✳✳✳

"In breaking news the notorious Cameron Forrest, wanted in connection with the death of five federal agents was killed today......"

"Grandma!" Cameisha wailed as the devastating news interrupted her regularly scheduled program.

"What's wrong girl?" Deidra asked concerned by her tone and rushed into the room. A grim faced reporter answered for the weeping girl.

"Last night agents raided a night club where Forrest along with reputed New York drug king pin Christopher Barnes were conducting a deal. An explosion of unknown origin claimed the lives of ten people, three of which were federal agents. Agents Nelson Ford, Adam Landry and Roland Anderson died during the raid. Some of the bodies have not been identified due to the extent of the fire ......"

"My son, My grandson" grandma Deidra whispered as tears warmed her cheeks. Cameisha came over and embraced her as they mourned their loss.

As they hugged and rocked agent Wilson took the podium and began to speak.

"We mourn the loss of three agents who bravely gave their lives in the war on drugs. Make no mistake, this is war....."

"I'm finna kill that man grandma" Cameisha vowed. She wasn't the only one making that pledge. A fugitive tucked away in his hideout made the same oath.

CHAPTER

48

C rystalline and her little crew mean mugged Cameisha and her grandmother as they walked to the store. Deidra glared back, her granddaughter chose to look elsewhere.

Elsewhere was the basketball court where a cute curly headed teen called Tay was showing out. He was shirtless and glistening in the sun and sweat. Cameisha still had an aversion to boys and didn't 'like' him, he was just nice to look at.

"I want you to go visit your Auntie Denise up in Yonkers this weekend" grandma announced out of the blue. She had just decided to add to all the other training the girl had received.

Deidra knew her grandson was teaching the girl the drug game, while her son no doubt taught her what he knew best. She had been in the streets long enough to know that she had raised a killer. She to had begun the over due process of teaching the girl how to be a lady. Now she needed to learn how to be a bitch.

Not a bitch in the bad sense of the word but a bad bitch in every good sense of the word. Aunt DG was just that.

"OK grandma" Cameisha said eager to please as usual. She had yet to meet her legendary aunt but assumed the sudden need to do so had something to do with the ugly girl talking shit about her loud enough to be heard.

"Un uh! This bitch does not have on white Capri pants with a white shirt!" Crystalline laughed prompting her flunkies to laugh along with her. Despite the fact the new girl looked cute.

Aqua fought the urge to ask what was wrong with matching but since her leader had on six different colors matching must be bad.

"And look how loose her shit is! Must ain't got no ass!" she laughed standing to prance her narrow ass around.

Deidra was livid, but Cameisha was still focused on the court. She smiled internally and what grandma didn't know. She had been secretly following Crystalline around since her father's death.

It took a little while to pin point which project unit she actually stayed in because she often went building to building delivering free pussy. Now all she had to do was wait. Wait for the malicious little bitch to give her a reason to kill her.

The thought brought to mind the old motel clerks head exploding. The satisfaction of killing him caused a wide smile to spread on her pretty face. She didn't necessarily like killing, but who wouldn't like killing someone who really, really deserves it. You gotta love that.

"I know that smile" grandma nodded knowingly. "Look just like my son when he got a job!"

"No job grandma" Cameisha lied unconvincingly.

"Lie just like him too"

Both Tay and Crystalline saw the smile and both thought it was for them. They were both right in a sense.

****

"We got the whole city to ourselves!" Nard cheered to his passenger agent B-large. "You're a fucking genius! Not only did you get rid of all competition but locked in a good price with the Mexicans. Most of all killed Cams bitch ass".

"Well, no more comp, and the Mexicans are fucking with us the long way, but uh...... Cam ain't dead" the agent replied.

"Huh? But the news said...."

"The news said what we, the government told them to say. The DNA came back to his father not him. None of it was his, he wasn't there!"

"Fuck! That nigga is gonna come hunting for me! You too!" Nard whined unable to mask his fear.

"Trust me, the last thing you have to worry about is Cam getting to you. You have my personal assurance he won't touch you" the agent said.

"Cool cuz that dude is a beast"

"That may be true, but there are people far worse" B-large replied referring to himself. "Pull behind that charger right there".

As Nard complied to the command B-large discreetly pulled a silenced pistol from his side. Once Nard stopped and put the car in park he turned to his friend just in time to see the flash that sent him rushing into the afterlife.

The driver in the charger just laughed as he watched the murder from the rear view mirror. The agent used a handkerchief to open the door and got out.

"Home James" B-large chuckled as they pulled away from the crime scene. 'He' not 'We' now had the city to himself.

✳✳✳

"Damn it, how did I forget the eggs!" Deidra fussed as she checked her bags. "Can't make macaroni and cheese without eggs"

"I'll run back and get some" Cameisha offered.

"Let me put my shoes on. I'll go with you".

"I can go by myself, I'll be OK" Cameisha insisted.

"Are you sure?" grandma asked knowing the Hood rats were at their post.

"I gotta go to school soon and you can't come there either you know?"

"I will you know!" Deidra laughed, "OK just, be careful"

"I will" Cameisha replied grabbing the news paper as she left. Grandma knew what the paper was for, her son taught her that too. A huge smile appeared as she rushed to the window to see the action.

"There she go right there, and she alone!" Angle announced happily. This was the moment they were waiting on.

"I'm bout to step to this bitch for trying me. Come on Angel!" Crystalline demanded.

The basketball game came to an abrupt halt as the boys watched the impending show down.

Too bad you gotta read Dope Girl to find out what happens......NEXT

EPILOGUE

A gent Wilson unlocked his door and entered his darkened home. He immediately secured the locks to his fortress and ventured in. He wasn't the least bit scared of Cam but precautions had to be taken, the man was dangerous. A creature of habit Wilson walked in the dark to his den where a snifter of brandy awaited.

"Hmp?" he questions when the switch failed to illuminate the pitch black room.

"I took the bulb out" an intruder announced from across the room in the agents comfortable recliner.

"For you to be in my house I assume you have a weapon pointed at me?" the agent asked.

"A fucking Canon!" the man replied with a laugh, racking the huge pistol as an exclamation point.

"S&W desert eagle 50 Cal." the weapons expert replied hearing the familiar slide and large round hitting the floor. "My only question is, why are you here?

"Really?" the intruder laughed.

"Well to kill me obviously, but why? The world thinks Cameron Forrest is dead. You're good, I'll give you that. We didn't even know about your dad until the DNA came back.

I suppressed it, no one knows your alive. I got a hundred large in my sa..."

"Ninety eight" the gunman corrected letting him know he had the money already.

"So go! Just go Cam, you won!" Wilson pleaded.

"That sounds like a plan, only I ain't Cam"

"Who the hell are you then?" Wilson barked, ready to try his luck going for his own gun.

"My name is Xavier" he said hitting the light, "but everyone calls me Killa"

Five rounds from the most powerful handgun on the planet blew chunks out of the crooked cop ruining his plans for the evening and forever.

Dope Girl

My father was Cameron Forrest, the illest dope boy ever. When other kids his age were still pissing in their pants he was hustling. A millionaire by age 21.

My grandfather was a hit man so deadly his name alone once killed a man. Dude heard who was on his ass and had a fatal heart attack. Keeled over dead just like that.

They weren't in my life long but they taught me all the skills I would need to survive. They wanted a better life for me and steered me to college. They made me promise to save my talents for rainy days.

But guess what? It's about to rain!